Girl on a Layover

A Steamy, Feel-Good, Second Chance Romance Novella

Cassandra O'Leary

Editor: Liz Dempsey at **https://theerroreliminator.wordpress.com**

Cover design: Deborah Bradseth at **https://www.dbcoverdesign.com**

Interior book design: Cassandra O'Leary, created with Atticus

Cassandra O'Leary, Author

Melbourne, Australia

cassandraolearyauthor.com

Blurg

Yuki Yamimoto has a problem with billionaires. If only she wasn't stuck in a luxury resort with one billionaire in particular!

Yuki agrees to be her friend Sinead's bridesmaid at her second wedding in a heartbeat. She's a flight attendant and used to jetting around the world, but staying at a luxury resort in Thailand for Sinead and Gabriel's renewal of vows sounds amazing – like a mini vacation. The only problem is. . . Declan Moriarty.

Years ago, Yuki and Declan shared a mind-blowing one-night stand and a few weeks of bliss, and then nothing. Nada. Was it all a dream? Or a nightmare? Because he cheated on her with his ex-fiancée and Yuki left before he could break her heart. Declan was Yuki's big fish, the one who got away. An Irish IT geek and billionaire built like a pro rugby player with bonus soulful blue eyes and dark wavy hair.

Yuki has a sinking feeling Declan will also be at the resort for the wedding celebration. Declan is a good friend of Gabriel's after all. But she won't have to hang out with him, surely? Yuki doesn't believe in second chances anymore. Besides, Yuki's just been dumped and humiliated and all she wants is rest and relaxation on this layover.

Declan no longer believes in love. In fact, he's probably cursed. Yuki isn't the only woman who ran from him or broke his heart. When he sees Yuki at the airport, he can't take his eyes off her. She's as gorgeous as ever. Maybe his luck is changing. Another fling might be just what fate has in mind!

A feel-good, second chance romcom novella with steamy scenes. And a monkey.

This book is #2 in the Girl on a Plane series by Cassandra O'Leary.

Contents

Chapter One

Destination: Thailand

Yuki Yamimoto had a problem with billionaires. Okay, with one billionaire in particular. She knew it, her friend Sinead knew it, and Yuki's entire flight crew had been briefed on the situation. On the off chance that there might be any princes, playboys, or powerbrokers on her flights, she'd always check out the passenger lists and obsess. But the one she obsessed over was never on board.

She glanced around the cabin now, clocking the faces of the other passengers as she tried to relax and enjoy her flight. While some flyers worried about engine trouble, Yuki worried about seeing *him*. Downtime was meant to be savoured and enjoyed. But she couldn't help being nervous, even as a passenger jetting off to a luxury resort for a long weekend.

It would be fair to say that Yuki fangirled over business moguls the same way other girls did over pop stars. She had a digital scrapbook packed full of articles on business wheeling and dealing she barely cared about, except for the images of one particular man. One gorgeous but slightly nerdy Irish IT mogul. The one who had broken her heart. *The One*. Maybe.

Best not to think about it...

Broken heart or not, she couldn't stop studying his photos. It was getting embarrassing. Especially at work, when waiting on the high-flyers hand and foot as a flight attendant in First Class. Everyone knew she had a gorgeous, high-profile boyfriend of her own, so it was weird to be so obsessed with a man from her past.

Correction: *had* a gorgeous boyfriend. Past tense.

Stupid, Yuki. Aim high, but not stratospheric. Stay in your lane.

Now that she was on break for a few days, it was time to unwind and get her head on straight. But unwinding would be challenging after the past few days. Her facial muscles contracted into a frown, the type that would give her wrinkles before she hit thirty. She breathed out slowly.

Still, Yuki's heart raced as she sat up rigidly in her cramped Economy seat. Turning to her right, she let her gaze wander to the world outside the plane. The clouds whooshed by her window before clearing to blue skies.

It would be hot in Thailand. Steamy. Normally, she enjoyed relaxing in the tropics—chilling at the beach and drinking cocktails. Not this time. This time she was attending a wedding, of sorts. When Yuki's own heart was fractured, this seemed a cruel and unusual punishment. She was only doing it for Sinead.

Yuki picked up her phone and scrolled through her messages again. Sinead's text message invitation had been a strange mixture of formal seriousness and bubbly excitement—confirmation that Sinead and Gabriel had composed it together (Gabriel being the serious-slash-grumpy one, and Sinead consisting of about ninety-nine per cent sparkles).

Dear Yuki,

You are cordially invited to the second wedding of Ms Sinead Kennealy, the world's funnest and prettiest former flight attendant,

and

Mr Gabriel Anderson, grumpy but gorgeous director of Global Village.

The bride and groom request the pleasure of your company
and to act as a witness to their nuptials, to be held at the
Elysium Resort, Thailand.
Exciting!
Please reply ASAP by return text. Your flights and accom-
modation are all taken care of so you can relax and enjoy! :)
P.S. sorry about the short notice!

They'd also included some bare-bones information about the time and the date. Abridged version of the fairy-tale: Sinead was in love with and married a billionaire, or at least millionaire. Gabriel was stupid-rich and stupid in love with Sinead. Married already for five years now, they were still as starry-eyed as ever. Gabriel obviously adored Sinead, or he wouldn't have agreed to a quickie wedding on the beach in Thailand in the first place, let alone a reenactment for their anniversary.

It was all so wonderful and romantic, and so sickly sweet that it made Yuki's teeth ache, like that time she'd eaten a whole bowl of M&M's at a celebrity party she'd attended with her ex. Yuki had hidden in the corner, scoffing the chocolate while he ignored her to flirt with supermodels. She'd felt sick—for multiple reasons.

Best not to think about it...

She dropped her phone in her lap and commenced moping, flicking through the in-flight magazine with no real interest in the pretty pictures of hotels and duty-free jewellery. Her eyes glazed over after a while, so she turned to stare out the plane's window, seeing nothing but blue sky and fluffy white clouds.

"Excuse me, ma'am, would you like any refreshments?" The woman's soft voice came out of nowhere.

Yuki glanced across to the aisle and the source of that question. Oh God, she'd been *Ma'amed*, and by a flight attendant about her own age. It was as if she'd aged a century over the past three days, and now she was no longer a *Miss* but a *Ma'am*. She could cry, except it would ruin her makeup.

Her horror must have been written all over her face because the pretty Thai flight attendant named Lucy leaned in and said, "Sorry to disturb you, Miss. Are you...? I think I know you. Oh, you're Sad Ex-Girlfriend!" Lucy pressed one hand to her mouth.

Yuki nodded, three times, rapidly. "Yep. That's me. I'm a meme! Please don't talk about it." She whispered the last part, whipping her head around to check no one else was listening in on their conversation. So far, it appeared the coast was clear.

"I'm sorry. Are you alright? Yuki, isn't it?"

"Yes, I'm fine. I'll be fine. Great. Probably." She shook her head.

The rambling wasn't a good sign. Her mental and physical collapse seemed imminent. But she needed to make it to her hotel room before she had a proper cry. "I'll take a sparkling mineral water. Thanks." She choked out the last word on a sob.

Lucy backed away slowly, perhaps worried she'd have to call the air marshals to lock up Yuki for the rest of the flight. It might be for the best. Keep her away from polite society and happy people.

Yuki didn't know what had gotten into her. Usually, she was an excellent traveller. Calm, organised, and happy to check into whatever three-star-or-higher hotel awaited her. Adventure was basically her middle name. This time, not so much.

She gripped the armrests of her "commoner class" seat, as she referred to it in her daily work as a flight attendant, and glanced down at her hands. Her French manicure was on point, the diamond Me Ring she wore on her right hand shiny and blingtastic.

But she was alone: facts were facts. She'd left her boyfriend, Daniel—no, correction, *ex-boyfriend*—behind in Singapore. And good riddance to bad rubbish. Okay, they'd had some good times. Incredible sex, at least at the beginning, *when* they managed to get together. Looking back on it, he was always meeting her in hotels and then flitting off somewhere.

Of course he'd had another woman on the side, probably more than one. Yuki closed her eyes and groaned. How could she have been so gullible? So trusting?

Daniel was a surgeon in training when they met, destined to be a big deal someday. Just not her Big Deal. The tosser had two-timed her with a female billionaire (the irony, it burned!) heiress to a Southeast-Asian noodle franchise. Now Daniel was engaged to her, and Yuki was officially dumped. And she wasn't getting any younger... twenty-seven next month, not that it paid to advertise the fact.

All these reasons could have explained why she was so nervous about flying into Thailand for Sinead's impromptu second wedding to online travel company director and all-round hottie Gabriel Anderson.

Reasonable explanation was reasonable.

She had to pretend to be happy, soak up the romance, and smile. Only, she didn't think any of those reasons were what had her all riled up. The billionaires and other fancy folk were no doubt seated at the front of this very plane, sipping champagne or top-shelf whiskey and nitpicking at girls like her, forced to serve drinks at ten thousand feet just to make a living.

One of those fancy folks could well be *him*. Her potential Big Deal from when she was a baby hotel receptionist with training wheels back in Melbourne.

Declan Moriarty, *her* Declan, was the real reason behind her infatuation with rich and powerful men. An app developer, IT guru, business owner, tech blogger, author, dead-set gorgeous bachelor, and generally great guy, he'd been her first love.

He'd let her go years ago without so much as a goodbye phone call or online friend request. But she still thought of him: his dark Irish good looks, his mesmerising brogue, cheeky grin, and dancing eyes, the way he kissed... not to mention when she'd got him alone in her bedroom.

Right now, she had a horrible feeling, a creeping sensation down the back of her neck, a tightening in her belly. She'd lay bets on Declan being one of the few guests at this second wedding. He and Gabriel were good friends; everyone knew that. They'd even been photographed together by the tabloids a few months ago, surfing in Byron Bay, Australia, when they were both taking a short vacation.

God, how she'd drooled over those photos of Declan, minus his shirt, plus an abundance of new muscles and suntan, standing astride a longboard, riding the crest of one of the biggest waves she'd ever seen.

Her face heated as she imagined meeting him again.

Touchdown, T-minus one hour.

Lucy, the flight attendant, returned at that moment with her mineral water, and Yuki nodded her thanks before gulping it down in barely three swallows. As her guts groaned and rebelled, the grilled salmon meal she'd scoffed earlier no longer seemed like such a good idea. Where was the sick bag?

Yuki grabbed the paper bag from the seat back pocket in front of her, shoved it over her mouth and breathed into it, concentrating hard.

Even if she did see Declan at the wedding, it wasn't like she had to talk to him. She could call him a bastard and storm off. Or shoot him. Would Sinead have a gun? Probably not. She'd have to acquire a lead pipe or a baseball bat instead. Easy-peasy. But jail time was a seriously bad idea.

Knowing her, she'd probably call him a bastard, then kiss him. The way Declan kissed was something else. Six years, and she hadn't experienced another kiss like it. Her stomach clenched—whether in pleasure or pain, she couldn't tell. Oh no, she was going to be sick...

Do not vomit. Do not vomit.

Yuki dry heaved instead. Like a pro.

Declan Moriarty was on a plane, headed to a vow renewal ceremony for his sins. He closed his eyes and sank back in his Business Class seat with a groan, taking a sip of surprisingly good whiskey.

Gabriel was a close friend, so Declan had decided to suck it up and zip across to Thailand for the man's impromptu wedding. Of course he'd agreed to be a witness at the last minute. He'd fly in, do the wedding thing, and be back home before he could blink.

Only it didn't feel like a small thing. It felt monumental, like a giant looming over him, about to crush him beneath its heavy feet. The sort of favour you didn't ask a friend without considering all its ramifications. And there were plenty of reasons why him going to this thing was a shite idea.

His conversation with Gabe two days ago had gone something like this:

"Mate, I'm getting married again."

Declan's eyes bulged until they achieved full bug-out status; he spluttered hard but tried to muffle the sound by turning it into a cough against his fist. "You're so full of it. Who's the lucky woman?"

His friend sighed over the phone. "Sinead. Irish. Former flight attendant and now travel consultant. Long platinum-blonde hair, the sweetest laugh in the whole world, and the woman I love. The only one for me."

Gabriel must have sensed Declan's confusion through the stunned silence because he continued, "I know we're already married. What can I say? It's true love. One hundred per cent. We wanted to do something special for our fifth anniversary."

"Well, then... congratulations?" He hadn't meant it as a question, but it came out that way as he shook his head. Gabe getting married again to the same woman was the most ludicrous thing he'd ever heard. And he'd once listened to a mate at business school pitch for green eco-rubber condoms shaped like frogs.

"I want you to be a witness. Come to Thailand. Beach wedding, no fuss. It'll be fun."

He closed his eyes, trying to imagine himself having fun at their faux wedding. He tried but failed. "I'd love to. Really. But you know what I'm like; me and weddings don't mix. I'll bring nothing but bad luck and destruction."

When he'd explained about the curse over the phone and tried to back out, his friend wouldn't hear of it. Not only that, but his happiness had somehow spread to Declan like a rash. He could only hope that love crap wasn't catching.

Declan had been left with no choice but to agree to take a few days off work and act as a witness at their wedding. Gabriel had been a great friend to him through all the ridiculous twists and turns of the past few years. His friend deserved to be happy, and Sinead was a good woman. Declan would support him on his big day, again, even if doing so all but killed Declan.

So, here he was, on a flight to Thailand. He stretched out his legs in front of him, his casual khaki pants and trainers looking out of place. Having drained his drink, he craned his neck and looked down the aisle for the flight attendant. There she was: Lucy. His fresh-faced purveyor of alcohol, aka liquid courage.

"Excuse me, Lucy-my-dear, could I trouble you for another whiskey, please?"

"Oh, of course, sir." She scuttled away behind a curtain, blushing to her ears. It was cute, in a casually entertaining way. Not that he had any interest in flirting.

Declan was a man of many talents, hidden and otherwise. Technically speaking, he was a certified genius. He didn't mean to be conceited about it—it was just there in his head, a talent for puzzles and numbers, systems, and data. IT code would bow down before him, no questions asked. Business-wise, he used this talent to his advantage, spotting trends and investing in various stocks and bonds, cashing in before the general public.

He could also flirt and schmooze with the best of them, mingle with the higher echelons of society or chat with whoever he met on his travels. He had a talent for attracting women too. Again, no conceit. To be honest, sometimes his Irish charm was more trouble than it was worth.

Women tended to swarm around him at business events and functions, like bees to a honeypot, as his old mam would say. Not that he liked to think of himself as a honeypot, seeing it as more of a female euphemism, but there you go. Declan preferred to be left alone. He'd pretend to enjoy himself for the minimum acceptable time and then head off home.

Pretending to enjoy weddings, however? Another matter entirely. They were his curse, his cross to bear. Some would say he'd been lucky to escape being a groom himself. He'd tell them luck had nothing to do with it.

It had everything to do with the cheating, lying, scheming women out for everything they could get: his name, his soul, not to mention his money and possessions. He'd managed to escape in the nick of time, not once, but twice. And the last thing he wanted was to curse Gabriel's wedding.

Lucy returned with his beverage, and he murmured his thanks. She smiled down at him in a certain way, lashes lowered, a covert glance at his bare left hand, but he waved her away. Polite but firm.

Declan took a slug of whiskey and considered his situation. This trip was an obligation. He'd make the best of it, to be sure. But flirting was not on the agenda. With a shake of his head, he plonked down his drink and opened his laptop, perched on his tray table.

He went back to calculating the return on investment on his latest business acquisition, a chain of eco-resorts scattered through the Asia Pacific, in association with Gabriel's company. This would be one of his best deals yet. Fingers crossed. He didn't want to jinx it.

Declan rubbed his right palm against his trousers. It was itchy for some reason. He tried to remember if Irish superstition said that was lucky. Was money coming his way? Or was someone speaking ill of him?

With his luck in the field of love, it was probably some woman wishing him dead.

Chapter Two

Touchdown

Suvarnabhumi Airport, Thailand

Yuki rushed down the concourse in her sparkly sneakers, dragging her bright pink mini wheelie bag behind her. Luckily, she didn't have any checked luggage. Her little pastel-pink stretchy dress was rolled up in her hand luggage, along with her strappy silver sandals, a couple of swimsuits, skirts and tops, a tube of sunscreen and some makeup. She was free and easy!

But she was also running late for her hotel shuttle service. The plane had circled the airport before sitting on the tarmac for a long while, for no apparent reason other than to make her late and even more nervy. Okay, they had said something about high winds and banked-up flights, blah blah blah. No *good* reason.

She could be at the resort in under an hour, stripped out of her sensible pants and cropped T-shirt and in the pool by lunchtime. *Bing, bam, boom!*

First, she had to get through security. This was serious business in Thailand, with big scary signs everywhere about the government's zero tolerance for drug smuggling. Oh God. Had she left that packet of ibuprofen in her bag? Was that illegal here? Why didn't she know?

Yuki shuffled through the barriers without incident, then wandered about, looking for the shuttle bus area. She lined up beside plane-loads of other Australian holiday-makers, sweating drippily. It was hot. Sticky. So humid that her light makeup had turned to liquid on her face. She pulled her cotton T-shirt away from her back, where it stuck to her damp skin.

Then, another kind of heat crawled up the nape of her neck—the prickling heat of awareness that someone was watching her. Ever so slowly, Yuki swivelled her head to cast a glance over her left shoulder, then her right. Frazzled parents, screaming kids, backpackers... Something called to her to crane her neck and check ahead of the line of travellers. There!

Oh no. Oh nonononononoooo!

Was she right, or was she right? She was soooo right. Why did she always have to be right? There he was, as if she'd somehow imagined him back into existence, Declan casually leaning against a service desk near the tourist information stand full of brochures—cool, calm, collected, and... calling her name.

What the hell? How dare he? She pretended to be invisible, crouching down behind a Hawaiian shirt–wearing man with a terrible mullet haircut.

"Yuki? Yuki Yamimoto, is that you?" His voice was exactly the same: a deep, rolling caress that tickled something deep inside, something suspiciously like her ovaries. She'd always been a sucker for an Irish accent.

She sucked in a breath, only to have trouble getting the air into her lungs. Her vision darkened around the edges, like she was looking through a vintage photo filter on Instagram. The heat prickling her skin now turned to ice in her veins.

She didn't mean to yelp, didn't mean to slide downwards, but there was the nice, cool floor. So close to her overheated face.

"Yuki?"

Could it really be the girl he'd met all those years ago in Melbourne? That stupid but incredible time at that hotel. An amazing kiss, a reckless night, and a few incredible weeks afterwards that he'd never forgotten.

He was almost certain it was her. She looked older, obviously, more poised and put together now. Glamorous and beautiful, even in casual clothes. She slumped to the ground as he watched. "Ah, shite. Yuki!"

Declan rushed through a group of tourists wearing ridiculously oversized backpacks. With his own lightweight carry bag slung over one shoulder, he shoved his way through people and trolleys full of bags until he stood beside her.

An older Thai woman bent over Yuki, her salt-and-pepper hair in a neat bun at the back of her head. Yuki lay face-down in front of the woman, legs sprawled across the floor, and her bag tipped over on its side. The woman stepped back as Declan crouched beside her. "She's my friend."

Friend wasn't exactly the right word for it, but what could he say? They had a history. The older woman smiled and stepped back but kept a watchful eye as he set his bag down and lifted Yuki's head into the palm of his hand, turning her face towards him.

As he smoothed back the shiny black strands of hair from her face and watched the fan of her long, velvety eyelashes flutter, his world tilted sideways. Because it was definitely her, but she was even more achingly beautiful. Still a definite temptation.

"Yuki? Can you hear me?" His voice cracked, his throat clogged with something. *Whiskey and regrets*, the poetic side of his mind whispered. But that side of his mind tended towards total and utter bollocks, so he ignored its commentary.

Her eyelids fluttered open, and she blinked once, twice. Her rosy lips opened on a sigh. Declan leaned closer; he couldn't help himself. He was only a couple of inches away when she muttered, "Declan, you bastard. What a nightmare."

With a stammered apology, he stood up straight, stepped back, and offered his hand. Yuki took it, swearing under her breath as he helped her to her feet.

Declan let his gaze rove over her body, ostensibly to check she was okay and steady on her feet, but in reality, caving in to the urge to check out the petite but deadly curves he remembered so well. He glanced up again when she grunted in frustration.

"Eyes. Up here." She pointed to her face, then pulled her bag to her side. Gaze fixed on him, she crossed her arms over her chest, huffing adorably. He didn't miss how her own eyes shifted to his chest before coming to rest on his face.

"Right. I take it you're invited to Sinead and Gabriel's wedding thing too. Let's get going." Yuki turned and stormed off towards the exit, where chauffeurs and bus drivers, taxis and tuk-tuks were located.

Wait, where was she going? She'd only just passed out and thought she'd take off on him again at a breakneck pace?

He raised his voice to get her attention as he jogged after her. "Yuki, wait. Are you ill? Do you need anything? Water? A doctor? Do you need me?"

She stopped abruptly, turned to face him, and announced, "There are many things I need: a shower, a new apartment, a boyfriend who's not a cheater, mascara that's truly waterproof. But *you* are not on the list. Not even down at the very bottom below chocolate martinis that don't make you put on weight or vomit after dancing. But I would like some cold water, thank you."

Declan's eyes rolled northwards, somewhere under his cowlick, but he met her gaze again and managed a stern finger wag. "Wait here. Sit," he ordered, and, miracle of miracles, she obeyed.

He left Yuki on a bench seat beside a tour-booking desk and took off to the nearest vending machine. He wasn't abandoning her. Absolutely not. Never again.

Declan could go rot in whatever cold, dark place billionaires hung out after they chewed up and spat out women like herself. Women with no power, who were too young or too trusting, or foolish enough to believe in love at first sight. In her case, all of the above.

No way was she waiting for Declan. She'd find her own way to the resort and see him later, *if* she had to. Only when it was absolutely necessary for wedding-related purposes.

Yuki stood, but her stupid head swam in a way that wasn't pleasant and didn't remind her of a cool, blue swimming pool. It was more like her head was filled with lukewarm, chunky vegetable soup. She plonked her butt back down on the ugly seat and dropped her head between her knees.

Great. She probably had twenty-four-hour cancer, or a heart aneurysm, or a tropical disease with bleeding lungs and eyeballs. She'd die alone in an airport. This likely wouldn't surprise anyone, friends and family included. How sad.

"Right. I got you plain water and sparkling. I wasn't sure which you'd prefer." The deep voice spoke to her through a megaphone from some distant galaxy, penetrating through litres of pea soup. When she looked up to meet his gaze, his brow was furrowed with lines, like someone had run a fork across his forehead. Those lines were deeper than they used to be.

Yuki reached for the sparkling water, and her fingers brushed against his, just for a second. *Mistake!* The word blared inside her head, probably attempting to clear the remnants of pureed vegetable matter. She knew better than to touch this man, even if it was an accident. Her fingers tingled, the echo of his skin on hers sparking delicious electricity.

Years ago, he'd clouded her mind when he took her hand. Then she was lost in his gorgeous eyes and even more gorgeous voice when he spoke low and sweet in her ear. Urging her to give him a chance. To dance with him. To touch him.

Well, she'd not fall for his line in Irish charm again. No way, no how. Even if her fingers still tingled and her stomach flipped, like touching him was a ride on the best kind of dangerous rollercoaster.

Yuki batted her eyelashes at him, the flirty move almost a reflex. "Thank you." *Dammit.* She shouldn't use that husky voice, either. But she couldn't seem to speak properly.

Declan's lips turned up at the corners. He had such pretty lips. And his eyes sparkled. A lot. He cleared his throat. "Um, sure. Do you think you can make it out to the street? We have a limo waiting."

"Limo? But the shuttle bus..." She waved her hand towards the buses lined up outside. "Wait... *we* have a limo waiting? As in both of us? Together?"

"Yes, us, the two people here, in this general vicinity. Gabe organised it and messaged me. You can't say no to the groom. So I guess you're stuck with me." He smiled: a wolfish, self-satisfied grin that had her insides heating in a way that had nothing to do with the ambient temperature.

It had everything to do with hormones and attraction and a raw sex appeal that had been missing, even with her last, quite-good-in-the-sack-thank-you-very-much boyfriend. She'd tried for years not to listen to that little voice in the back of her mind telling her it had been so much better with Declan.

Yuki glanced up at him, and everything inside her tightened in a familiar, delicious way, as if he'd activated a secret code hidden deep in her blood. That little voice whispering about hot nights and twisted sheets.

Her body remembered him all too well. *Dammit.*

She shook her head. "Fine. Take me. I mean, take me with you. To the limo." Yuki out a groan as she got to her feet.

Declan's chuckle echoed in her ears as she followed him.

Chapter Three

Roadblock

By the time Declan had Yuki beside him in the back of the limo, her huffing and rolling her eyes at him, he was thoroughly entertained, not to mention more than a little turned on. She crossed her legs and turned to stare out the window, and he let out a genuine laugh. She wouldn't even deign to look at him anymore.

Declan appreciated a woman who hated him; it was true. Some people would call it a character flaw, but they would be idiots. Because of all the women who'd professed to like him, let alone love him, over the years, close to one hundred per cent had turned out to be the worst kind of cold-hearted mercenaries.

He could do without women who pretended to like him while calculating exactly how much he'd be worth in a future divorce settlement. No, straight-up loathing with an edge of feral sexual attraction was more his speed.

Hate sex has its benefits.

A cascade of images tumbled through his head, most starring the woman pretending to ignore him seated to his right. But in his head, she was stripped naked, those slim legs wrapped around his waist, her ragged sighs and moans spurring him on. Making him so hard that he was practically a statue.

He stared out the window on his side of the limo with a focused concentration, counting palm trees on the side of the road as they passed by. Before long, they were out of the city, passing through tiny villages and a small market town featuring colourful temples, bars, and even a convenience store. This peninsula wasn't exactly the ends of the earth, more a destination for travellers who liked to relax a little off the beaten track.

Declan leaned forward to open the door of the in-built bar fridge and pulled out two mini bottles of water. He waved one in her direction. "Here, you might be needing this. You looked like you might hurl back there in the airport."

Not the smoothest of conversation starters, true. "You two-faced, low-life, scum-sucking... barnacle of a man. Don't you dare talk to me as if we're happy strangers sharing a ride to the resort! I'm an actual person with actual, real memories, you know. You can't go around doing... what you did... without consequences."

Declan wasn't sure what he'd done to deserve the barrage of abuse Yuki threw his way.

The muscle in his forehead that controlled his wacky left eyebrow went a little mad, twitching as it tugged upwards. What the hell was she talking about? What exactly had he done to her? This angry but admittedly still extremely sexy woman, full of fire and fury, was looking at him like she'd burn him to dust with her stare.

His memories of Yuki were a sort of fever dream, a Christmas down under, back when he was free, his business responsibilities not yet making life impossible. Dancing beneath glittering stars, a kiss that shredded brain cells, soft, satiny lips, those dark eyes that reflected the galaxy an assault on his senses. Silky strands of her hair between his fingers, the scent of her shampoo, something like mint and rosemary. Good enough to eat.

Then, in his hotel room, the two of them pressed close, tangled up in each other, the taste of her... Yes, she'd made an impression. For a few glorious weeks, they were everything to each other. He hadn't wanted to end things, but circumstances had been out of his control. Clearly, he'd never forgotten her.

Declan swallowed on a dry throat and leaned back in the leather seat of the limo, stretching his legs out in front of him. Truth be told, his cargos felt a little constrictive in the crotch region. His gaze flicked to Yuki's face, and he caught a touch of blush colouring her cheeks.

He cleared his throat and muttered, "I don't know what I did to make you so mad at me, but to be honest, it's turning me on."

Yuki snorted. "You don't know."

"No. Not a clue."

"You expect me to believe that? Considering the phone call that morning in London. After we... after our night together." She shook her head and turned away.

Phone call? Declan racked his brain for details but came up with nothing. It must have been his assistant. She was the only person he could remember talking to that day, apart from Yuki, of course. He'd been in no mood to talk to anyone else after the nightmare of the day before.

They'd been staying together in a hotel in London. She'd been training as a flight attendant, and he'd had a string of meetings he wanted to forget. But now that he thought back, Yuki had gone cold on him after their tasty breakfast in bed. She'd told him she needed to get back to Australia, thousands of miles away, and left.

Her whole manner had been off. And when he'd tried to call her that night, the phone number didn't connect. She hadn't been on social media or anywhere online. The Yuki trail had gone stone cold. The next time he visited Melbourne, he'd swung by her apartment but found she'd moved out, and her flatmate couldn't tell him where she'd gone. Yuki had disappeared without explanation, without a trace. He'd assumed she'd happily moved on without him because, in his experience, that's what women did when they left him.

God, she'd ghosted him. He'd been a fool not to see it. But why? Hadn't they had fun? More than fun. She'd been a passionate, wild woman in bed. As for him? He'd let himself go in a way he hadn't for years. He'd fallen for her.

Declan glanced at her across the limo seat and caught her accusatory stare. "I'm sorry if I hurt you. It was seriously unintentional."

She made a sound low in her throat, like a growl, and he braced himself for another torrent of abuse. But instead, her eyes went wide as she stopped on the verge of saying something and nodded instead.

"I don't want to talk about it anymore. We're here for Sinead and Gabriel, to celebrate their love with them. Any history between us"—she gestured wildly from her chest towards his—"stays behind closed doors. They don't need us being Debbie Downers and raining on their parade."

Declan's errant eyebrow did its twitchy thing again. Yuki clocked the motion and crossed her legs, apparently awaiting his response.

She was being reasonable. That was unexpected. Women usually went off at him at some point about him being too wrapped up in his work, not spending enough time with them, failing to remember their birthdays, being late to dinner dates, and so on. He wasn't prepared for a woman who was obviously angry, perhaps even hurt, but decided not to throw a Molotov cocktail of emotions at him.

He extended his right hand for her to shake. "Truce?"

Yuki pursed her lips and hesitated, her hand hovering above her knee. Suddenly, she thrust it forward and grabbed his hand. "For now."

Sparks exploded at every point where their palms touched. The heat, the intensity of it, had him sucking in a breath, sitting straighter. The effect this woman had on him, the feel of her skin, even the touch of her hand, had him burning with need. This was what he remembered. Pure, unadulterated *want*.

He still wanted her. And, from the look on her face—a dawning realisation of something *more*, something vivid and alive and real between them—it was only a matter of when they'd collide. No ifs, buts, or maybes. Well, probably some butts.

The limo jolted to a sudden halt with a screech of brakes. Declan jerked forward and only just managed to grab Yuki's forearm before she slammed to the floor.

She slowly raised herself back onto the seat and smoothed down her shirt. It had ridden up her stomach, revealing a tantalising glimpse of skin. Satiny skin that he wanted to taste.

Declan cleared his throat for about the hundredth time since meeting her again. "I guess we're here."

Yuki peered out the car's side window and squealed. "Oh wow, monkeys!"

"Monkeys?" What the devil was she on about? He peered around her shoulder to look out her window.

Sure enough, there *were* monkeys. A bunch of the furry creatures sat beside the road at a roadside stall. The cheeky brown-and-white fellas sat on top of a box full of bananas, happily sampling the merchandise while a stall keeper jumped around, madly trying to wave them away.

They'd stopped on the street adjoining the driveway into their resort—the large steel gates may have been partly to keep out the local wildlife. Gabriel had mentioned the place was exclusive, meaning pricey, but it appeared it was also a high-security enclave. That made sense, given that Gabriel was something of a public figure these days. As was Declan, for that matter.

The limo driver leaned around the edge of his seat. "Sir, ma'am, we have arrived, but we must wait for the road to clear." He pointed towards the windscreen.

Declan assumed he was referring to the monkeys. Until his gaze followed the man's finger. He was pointing to a group of people and a particularly large brown cow stopped right in the middle of the road. A natural roadblock, if you will.

With a chuckle, he touched Yuki's forearm to get her attention. Her skin was warm beneath his fingertips. He snatched his hand away immediately. "Apparently, monkeys aren't the only wildlife to contend with around here."

She swung around to face forward and burst out laughing at the sight. "Monkeys and cows and bananas, oh my!" Her face lit up, transforming her into a different woman. Younger, carefree. Gorgeous.

Their driver jumped out of the vehicle and approached the group standing in the middle of the unpaved road. One of the younger men was trying to push the cow forward with both hands planted on the cow's wide derriere, putting his full body weight behind the job. This provoked a loud *moo*, but that was all. No moving, no getting out of their way.

The gathered crowd shouted and laughed, including their limo driver, who looked more flustered than anyone. He held his cap in one hand while rubbing the other through his short black hair.

Declan watched as the main cow pusher stepped back, clearly exhausted. "That poor lad's struggling. I might give him a hand."

He jumped out and rounded the front of the vehicle. Once he made it into the road and the vicinity of the cow, he introduced himself to the main wrangler, the young man named Somsak. After shaking his hand, Declan cracked his knuckles and joined in the pushing.

"There you go, Daisy, there's a good girl." He spoke quietly as he pushed, and although he didn't know her actual name, Daisy seemed a good guess.

The cow was obstinate; that's all there was to it. His hands spread, palms flat on bovine buttocks, he gave another great push with all his might.

"Stop, wait!" Yuki yelled over the collective noise of the gathered men. The cow at the centre of the events let out another *moooo* that was lower pitched, sounding quite put out.

Tracking her voice, Declan glanced around one large animal flank. When he located her, Yuki was racing out into the road ahead of the cow, phone in hand. She tilted her head to one side, lining up her phone camera to get the cow in shot.

Wait... photos? Now? Oh, God help him. Was Yuki a social media addict like Callista, one of his ex-girlfriends? No way did he need more stupid personal photos online. He's been waiting for the bomb to drop from Cal's last load of happy snaps, which she most likely shopped around to the paparazzi. He hoped the photos were too old to be of interest now. Still, he'd been stupid to trust her. He'd not make that same mistake again.

Declan rushed around the cow's starboard side but tripped over another guy's feet as he went and tumbled face-first into the mud. But he wouldn't be stopped, oh no, because one glance up at Yuki revealed a face-splitting grin as she giggled and snapped yet more photos of his face-plant.

"Oh no you don't, missy!" Declan pushed off the ground and launched himself in her direction. He swiped at the phone before properly righting himself and only succeeded in grabbing Yuki's elbow, pulling her off-balance.

That's when the monkey appeared.

One of the little scamps climbed straight up Declan's leg, balanced on his forearm, and leaned over to snatch the phone clean out of her hand. With an answering screech to Yuki's squeal, the monkey scrambled down and away.

"Hey!" she shouted, but it was no use. That monkey wasn't about to stop.

Declan broke into a jog and followed the monkey into the trees lining the side of the road, heading off to who knew where.

Yuki waited in the middle of the road for at least twenty minutes while the cow was ushered away, before asking the limo driver to take her to the resort. They pulled up outside its main entrance, minus one annoying Irishman with too much money and arrogance to spare. And her phone. That was still missing in action, presumed dead or in the clutches of a primate on the run.

The hotel, or rather six-star resort, stretched out at her feet like a palace as she stepped from the limo. Marble columns met thatched roofs while carved wooden seats and jewel-coloured silk draperies embossed with what appeared to be gold leaf adorned the reception area.

A hotel staff member named Annie, with shiny black hair worn in a sleek bob and a matching sleek black suit, ushered her into reception. Really, it was more of a semi-outdoor waiting room, but she was waiting for what? Possibly the King of Siam to ride in on an elephant. Or for Declan. Probably not on an elephant.

Yuki had missed Declan, painful as that was to admit. It had been years since she'd seen him in real life. Online stalking didn't count. He was still ridiculously handsome, his thirties fitting him like a perfectly tailored suit.

Seated in a cane chair with silk cushions, she sipped her welcome drink of mango and lychee juice, complete with paper straw and little umbrella. Delicious. Just like Declan.

Yuki gaped as he strolled in, cool as the proverbial cucumber in fresh khaki pants and a loose white shirt left partly open. It revealed a tantalising glimpse of chest and dark hair that, honest to God, made her want to worship him. Or at least lick him around the pecs area. But when did he get changed?

"We meet again, my young friend," Declan announced in a deep voice.

He didn't mean to put on Jedi Master airs, surely. There was only six years between them, which was hardly anything at all in the scheme of things. Except maybe he'd found her too immature when they first met. She shook her head, attempting to dislodge thoughts of how they'd messed up their relationship, or fling, or whatever it was back then. It was in the past. Daniel, her ex-boyfriend, would have said it was all due to Yuki's immaturity. Declan wouldn't say something like that.

She nodded to him as he loped towards her. "Hi."

Declan tipped his chin in her direction. "Thought you'd abandon me while I chased a monkey on your behalf, did you? Because that sounds like the start of an interesting story." He grinned, and, wow, he lit up. His eyes legit twinkled. "Sorry, I didn't find your phone."

She exhaled slowly. Maybe she was trying to calm her raging hormones, or perhaps she was just tired. It had been a rough week. "Right. I didn't know what you were going to do. It got too hot standing out there in the sun."

His forehead crinkled. "Are you feeling alright now?"

Yuki shrugged. "Just tired, I guess. I have a bit of a headache."

Declan was suddenly right there in front of her, leaning down and stroking his thumb along her jawline, lifting her gaze to his. He scanned her face, but looking for what?

"Follow my finger." He pointed upwards with his index finger, moving his hand from right to left. "You could have a concussion. I can't believe I didn't think to check earlier."

Yuki shook her head. "What are you talking about?"

His fingers glided over her forehead, and she shivered. He met her eyes, his gaze filled with concern. "At the airport. When you fell, you might have hit your head on the floor. Back when I played rugby, I saw more than one fella left with a concussion after hitting his head on the field."

She shook her head again, slowly this time, not wanting to rattle her brain any further. The idea was simply revolting. After the week she'd had, the thought of being sick or injured on her getaway at a luxury resort was enough to make her ill. Oh, the nausea...

Yuki pressed her lips together, then spoke in a croaky whisper: "I was feeling queasy, but that was before I hit my head."

He nodded once, then straightened, his hand extended in her direction. "Let's get you checked out. Surely a resort as fancy as this must have a doctor onsite, or at least nearby. Maybe down in the monkey village."

Yuki placed her hand in his, almost sighing at his warmth and strength, his large hand curled around hers. She'd always felt protected with him. Maybe it wouldn't be so bad to let Declan look after her, just for a little while.

Chapter Four

Project Relaxation

In her luxury cabin, Yuki lay back on her king-sized four-poster bed with its gorgeous white silk sheets and let out a long, shuddering breath. The local doctor, a friendly Swedish-Thai woman named Karin who'd put Yuki at ease, had just gone. Leaving her with strict instructions to relax, Karin said she'd call to check on her tomorrow.

Panic attacks. Who knew they could make a person feel so unwell? Doctor's orders were to avoid all unnecessary stress for a few days, to unplug and chill. She'd prescribed some anti-nausea tablets plus Valium in case Yuki needed them, but hopefully, her body would naturally unwind. She badly needed this break.

After emailing her supervisor, Yuki was now officially on leave from work for four days. She was perfectly understanding when she said she needed some personal time. Of course. Her private life was being aired all over the Asian media like so much dirty laundry. At this point, she'd just be disruptive on flights due to passengers stopping her to ask inappropriate questions.

This short getaway would be the perfect antidote for all of life's recent crap. If she could stay in her cabin most of the time, even better. Now that she thought about it, she didn't even want her phone back. It was old, and she didn't need to look at it for a while. A total social media detox seemed like a great idea.

A knock on the door had her sucking in a breath and sitting up in a rush. Her head spun in a sickening way. That wasn't good. Not good at all. She took a couple of long, cleansing breaths, and the room righted itself. "Hang on a minute."

"No problem. It's just me. Declan." Her belly did a somersault. She'd recognise that sexy Irish accent anywhere.

"Um, coming!" she called out.

Slowly, Yuki got to her feet and began making her way across the few metres to the door. She had to stop short and lean against the wall to catch her breath. She wasn't panicking exactly, but bubbles of nervous energy coursed through her body. It was totally annoying the effect Declan had on her.

She opened the door and sucked in a sharp breath as she took a step back. Declan dominated the doorway. Literally. He leaned in the doorframe like he owned it, nailed it, probably slapped it for good measure.

Wow. Yuki let out a strangled laugh. She was jealous of a doorway.

"Hi." His voice was a delicious mix of whiskey and honey. "So what did the doc say?"

"Oh." She shrugged, ushering him inside with one hand while keeping an eye on his biceps. The way they flexed as he pushed off the doorframe and stepped towards her was... distracting. "Apparently, I'm having panic attacks. Anxiety. You probably think that's pathetic."

Declan stopped mid-stride and put his hands on his hips, a furrow forming in the space between his dark eyebrows. "No. Don't do that. I don't know what's been going on with you, but stress, anxiety, it's real. I get how that shite can derail your life. Don't let anyone tell you it's not important. You just need to learn how to manage it."

Her mind going a mile a minute, she nodded. Declan understood way too much. "Thank you for saying so. I'm trying to get used to the idea that I don't have everything under control, but I guess no one does."

He folded his arms over his chest. "Ah. You're a wise woman these days, Yuki Yamimoto."

She didn't miss how his gaze flitted over her body. Although wrapped in the hotel's fluffy cotton robe, she felt all sorts of naked underneath. The actual sort, and also the raw, exposed, emotional sort she usually ran away from at the first hint of mushy emotions.

Yuki met Declan's eyes, and something stirred in the pit of her stomach. Something akin to "liking" but stronger. She didn't want to think about it. "Um, thanks. I'd better rest now. Doctor's orders."

When he nodded and left with a quiet goodbye, Yuki leaned against the closed door and let out a long, slow breath.

Obviously, Declan Moriarty was too much for her system to handle.

Later, Declan rapped lightly on Yuki's cabin door, knowing he probably shouldn't bother her again. Still, it had been a while, and if she was anything like him, she wouldn't want too long a nap. It would mess up her body clock. Also, he was worried about her. But in a casual, friendly way, that was all.

His own problem was quite ridiculous: Declan was bored. He'd admit it. Gabe and Sinead hadn't appeared yet, and as far as he was aware, no one else in their group had arrived at the resort. He'd already been swimming at the private beach, had a drink at the bar, and started reading a thriller that didn't hold his attention. It hadn't been long before he'd logged in to his work email and caught up on business.

Declan was determined not to work too much this weekend. He was supposed to be scaling down. He had assistants and managers aplenty these days, who could easily hold the fort while he was travelling. He had no interest in working himself into an early grave, which was exactly why he'd sold off a large chunk of his business. Now he had more time on his hands and needed to get a life.

Before he'd consciously decided or even told his feet which direction to head in, he'd been staring at Yuki's cabin door.

He knocked again, more forcefully this time.

"Yuki? Are you awake? Just wondering if you'd like to grab a bite to eat." He hadn't really given food much thought, but it was getting late for lunch, and surely Yuki wouldn't want to sleep through restaurant opening hours.

"Um, Declan?" The words, muffled through the door, were hesitant.

When she opened the door, she was adorably sleepy-looking, her hair tousled and her face pink. She'd never looked more attractive.

"Come with me. Let's see if we can find Sinead and Gabriel."

Declan was a sweet man; she'd always thought so. Sexy as sin too. Even when she'd cut off all contact to save her own heart, she hadn't stopped thinking about him. For a while, she'd wished she could block him from her mind, but no such luck. He was embedded in her brain, a core memory drenched in pleasure.

This time, she'd be careful. She wouldn't give him the power to break her heart again. It had already been poked and pummelled so much it hardly worked. Except when it squeezed so tight in her chest that it was painful. Maybe that was the anxiety. *Whatever.*

As Declan tugged on her hand, she shook her head to get rid of the past, then accompanied him to the hotel reception area. They'd had a first look around the resort, but Declan thought they should wait for the bride and groom.

Yuki plonked herself down in another cane chair and went to grab her phone, usually located in her hip pocket. Of course it was still missing. She patted her empty pocket. "Ugh. I wanted to call Sinead to see where she and Gabriel are."

"Do you want me to try Gabe?" Declan's forehead crinkled adorably.

"Yes, please."

She scraped her fingers through her messy hair, then smoothed it down over her shoulders while Declan paced back and forth in front of her, phone pressed to his ear.

"He's not picking up. I'll try texting him."

Declan tapped out a message and sent it, but before she could even ask if Gabriel had replied, Sinead galloped into the reception area. Her friend was stunning—all long limbs and pale blonde hair, but the thing that Yuki noticed most was the smile that lit up her whole face. She looked positively radiant.

Yuki assumed it was all the happiness and great sex of married life basically oozing from her pores. Jealous? Her? Okay, maybe a little.

Sinead launched herself at Yuki and grabbed her by the shoulders. "Oh, there you are! My God, I've had a time of it finding you. The chauffeur said something about monkeys and cows. I think he might have sunstroke, to be honest. How are you?"

Her friend's last question was a muffled whisper, her face smooshed into Yuki's neck as she wrapped her in a hug. For some reason, it made Yuki want to cry and hide under her bedcovers.

Yuki shrugged, her breath escaping in a shudder. "I've had better weeks. Daniel dumped me, as you know. Now he's suddenly engaged to an heiress, the Singapore press is in meltdown, and I'm a meme! Sad Ex-Girlfriend. Someone posted a video of me crying, and it's gone viral. I had to escape. So... that's how I am."

Sinead squeaked out a sound of sympathy and patted her on the back, slowly and rhythmically. She murmured soothing words that, surprisingly, helped calm Yuki down.

Out of the corner of her eye, Yuki noticed Declan's attention on her from his position near a potted palm tree in the corner. She flicked a glance his way as she got to her feet and linked arms with her friend. She couldn't deal with him watching and judging her.

"I can tell you more over a drink," she said as she tugged Sinead towards the bar, an open-air affair in the middle of a gorgeous garden courtyard.

"Um, see you later, Declan," Yuki called back over her shoulder as an afterthought, but he'd already gone.

Declan slammed his cabin door shut behind him, then sank onto the bed and kicked off his trainers, two pertinent facts on his mind.

One: Yuki was very recently single. He had no idea who this Daniel character was, but the man sounded like a right arsehole. Imagine dumping a gorgeous and adorable girl like Yuki. Imagine wanting to marry anyone else.

Two: Yuki was going through something traumatic—in public—and it involved the press. Declan knew how that went. It was his worst nightmare come back to haunt him.

That his own ex had gushed like a fountain to the media about their private life and had him fired from a company he founded was common knowledge. What wasn't common knowledge was how Declan had reacted to the situation. Panic attacks and anxiety were his old friends, it was fair to say. Not to mention a terrible period of blackness when his depression became almost impossible to manage.

Although a part of him didn't want to do it, he grabbed his phone and scanned the Singapore newspaper headlines anyway. Declan had no intention of hurting Yuki any more than she'd already been hurt. However, he needed to know exactly what had happened to her. So he could help. Or at least offer a sympathetic ear.

And find out, he did. Daniel was a complete arse; he'd been right. Imagine a man taking his new fiancée to a red-carpet event, her baby belly on full display in a clinging evening gown, when only a week before, he'd been quoted as having no comment on his relationship with long-time girlfriend, Yuki Yamimoto. Previously he'd described them as "madly in love".

There were photos of Daniel and Yuki at a string of charity galas, yacht parties, fashion parades, and so on. She looked devastatingly beautiful, of course, if ever so slightly nervous in all the photos. He zoomed in on one photo in particular—Yuki, in a pink silk dress, holding a glass of champagne. If you didn't look too closely, you wouldn't notice how white her knuckles were where they gripped the glass. Or that her eyes were a fraction too wide.

Daniel was movie-star handsome, a high-profile surgeon, mixing with the movers and shakers. There was also something about his expression... In all the photos online, his smile was completely fake, never reaching his eyes. Did Yuki know the real man lurking beneath that smile?

A pounding on his door made him start before he sat up on the bed. "Fuck me! Who is it?" Swearing like a true Irishman. Hopefully he wouldn't offend the locals.

"Gabe. You okay, mate?" The male's voice was muffled by the wooden door.

Finally. His old friend would understand Declan's concerns about this whole fiasco. Well, probably. Gabriel did sometimes accuse him of overreacting to stressful situations.

When he opened the door, Gabriel stood in the doorway looking cool and composed, unlike Declan himself. Gabe's blue linen shirt and tan shorts were Aussie summer casual personified. He also appeared to be in a cheery mood, judging by the grin he shot Declan's way.

"Dec, what's with hiding out in your room? There's a beautiful beach and gorgeous women outside."

Ah, his time-to-cheer-up-Declan routine. An old favourite. He didn't begrudge Gabriel his happiness, but sometimes, Declan was just in a shitty mood. It was a bone of contention between them whether Declan should be allowed to be down in the dumps. Sometimes, the situation warranted a bloody good sulk. Or time to lie down and think.

Declan stepped back a pace and raised his phone, still held in his hand. "Right. Except I'm just learning about Yuki's ex, who seems like a complete tool."

Gabriel ran his fingers through his blond hair, messing it up. "Yeah, about that. I don't think you should mention it to her. Yuki's had a rough time of it lately, according to Sinead. She thought... that is, *we* decided, it would be good for Yuki to come here and lie low for a bit. She's got some time off work for the wedding and needs to relax. Somewhere safe."

With a long exhalation, Declan nodded. "Okay. But I'd have appreciated a warning that I was likely to run into her, though. You know we didn't leave things on the best note back in the day."

Gabriel gestured to the outside world, all sunshine and steamy heat, palm trees and blue skies. "Come on. Now that you're here, let's go have some fun. That pool's just begging for a cannonball."

Declan groaned. "How old are you? I swear, married life's made you even more immature."

Gabriel's chuckle was a good sign. He wasn't here to give Declan a hard time.

He studied his friend. The lines etched around his eyes had softened. Even though he'd been through a lot, he was looking well. "You're happy. Really, truly, stupidly in love. It's grand to see."

"Thanks, mate. So, how about that swim?"

The pool sparkled across the courtyard garden. Declan squinted and could make out Yuki and Sinead seated beside it, sipping cocktails. "Alright. You're on."

Chapter Five

Jump Right In

"Yuki, are you really alright? You can tell me," Sinead said in a lazy, sleepy voice as she sat on the edge of the pool, her feet dangling in the water. She glanced over the top of her oversized sunglasses, her platinum-blonde ponytail flicked over one shoulder, looking for all the world like a glamorous pop star.

"Yes, I'm good. Mmm, this drink is delicious." Yuki leaned back in her sun lounger and sucked another mouthful of daiquiri through a bamboo straw.

"We can go for a walk along the beach soon if you like." Sinead turned back to the pool, apparently content to watch the sway of palm trees and the family on the other side of the courtyard. A tubby little toddler and a baby played on a rug while their parents watched on proudly.

Yuki followed Sinead's gaze. More tourists sat on the other side of the pool. A man with ginger hair and a Hawaiian shirt made her smile as he looked so out of place, red-faced, reading a newspaper. He wandered off, probably going inside.

Yuki hummed her agreement at Sinead's suggestion, but she didn't have the energy to move yet. Warm sunlight bathed her skin, and with her sunglasses on, she saw the world bathed in a golden glow, like liquid honey. The tension in her muscles unwound like a spool of thread.

She couldn't remember the last time she'd sat in the sun, drinking a cocktail, without any place to be. It might have been when she visited Bali with Sinead many years ago. And wasn't that a sad reflection of her life as a twenty-something? She was supposed to be going out, having fun. At least, that's what everyone said she should be doing. Nights out on the town hadn't been fun for Yuki for quite some time.

While other women her age had been studying, building careers, moving in with their partners, getting engaged or even married, she'd been stuck. Sure, she'd flown around the world and seen some amazing places, but it was hard to put down roots as a flight attendant.

Then there was Daniel. Yuki had played his perfect trophy girlfriend for a while, being ushered around red carpets and soirees in mansions, being ignored by fancy people and listening to conversations she had no stake in. Most of the time, she'd have preferred to be at home, streaming Netflix in her pyjamas. And wasn't that a bizarre thing to realise?

Whenever she thought of Daniel now, it made her mad. He'd cheated on her in the most public way, and it was highly embarrassing. But also, she felt strangely relieved. She was rid of him. Finally, she was free.

Yuki wouldn't have to get Botox unless she wanted to (she didn't), and she wouldn't have to go to all those corporate mixers and chat with guys who thought they could buy her (they couldn't). While with Daniel, she'd received several weird offers and even an off-the-cuff proposal from a genuine sheikh. He'd been more than a little creepy.

Most importantly, she wouldn't have to pretend everything was okay while Daniel yelled at and belittled her behind the walls of his apartment, calling her flaky, immature, ridiculous. She'd no longer have to hide how her heart thundered around him, not from love, but from stress and anxiety.

A loud thundering sound woke her daydreamy self to her current surroundings. A flash of colour and movement in the corner of her eye made her turn seconds before an enormous splash in the pool in front of her made her squeal. Cold water hit her face, dripping down the front of her kaftan. With a splutter, she stood and shook herself off like a dog.

"What on earth…?" Yuki stared down at the man in the pool, surfacing and slicking his dark, wavy hair back from his face. "Declan. What is your problem?" She crossed her arms and glared at him.

He shot her a cheeky grin. "No problem, just having a little swim. The water's fine. You should try it." He trod water while speaking, giving her a tantalising view of his chest. It was very broad. And wet. Glistening, even.

Yuki shook her head. "Not if you're staring at me."

"Come on… Oh, watch out!" Declan shouted a moment too late because Gabriel had already jumped in, near where Sinead sat.

Her friend screamed, and fair enough, too, as she was totally saturated. Luckily, Sinead had worn a bikini under her shorts and blouse. She whipped off her wet clothes and tossed them onto an empty banana lounge, then lowered herself into the pool, slowly, gingerly… Gabriel swam towards her, grabbed her by the ankle, and yanked her into the water.

Watching from what she assumed was a safe distance, Yuki giggled, until she copped the full force of the splash when Sinead went in.

"Argh!" Yuki shook herself again, then peeled her soaked kaftan off over her head and flung it onto the banana lounge alongside her friend's discarded clothes. Her yellow bikini underneath was totally cute. "You guys, this wasn't on my holiday bingo card."

When she glanced over at Sinead and Gabriel, they weren't listening to her. They were joined at the lips, canoodling like a couple of love-sick teenagers.

A quick look at Declan revealed he wasn't paying the soon-to-be re-newlyweds any attention. He was staring at Yuki with an odd expression—a combination of lost puppy and starving man rolled into one. He blinked hard and seemed to come back to life.

"Care for a swim?" That cheeky, lopsided grin reappeared, an expression she loved.

No, strike that from the record! She *liked* it, not loved. A long time ago, she'd liked it. She closed her eyes for a second. For some reason, she'd gone all hot. Her face felt horribly sunburned. But she knew this heat came from inside her body.

Yuki reopened her eyes and shrugged. "Since I'm already wet..."

His face did that thing again, his mouth hanging open.

She tested the water with one foot, dipping her toes in the cool, blue water. While trying to ignore Declan, she strolled to the steps in the rounded corner of the lagoon-style pool and slowly inched her way down to waist level. For such a steamy day, the water was quite cool. But it was refreshing.

"Better?" Declan was watching her when she looked up.

She tipped her head to one side and studied him. Yep, still yummy. "Yes, I think I needed to cool off."

Yuki ducked under the water, getting in properly. She pushed off from the edge and swam a few lazy lengths of the pool, keeping away from Declan, and Sinead and Gabriel at the opposite end. The water skimmed over her body as she swam, and it was easy. It was like a different world beneath the water. So calm and peaceful.

When she stood up again, Declan had left the pool and was sitting on a chair near the lounger she'd occupied. Sinead and Gabriel were nowhere to be seen.

"Yuki, come sit by me."

Somehow, her legs were moving before she'd thought about it, and she was out of the pool, dripping wet, twisting her ponytail into a rope to squeeze out most of the water. While patting herself down with her towel, she tried not to look at Declan. She sensed he was still watching her, and secretly, she liked it.

He'd always told her she was hot, beautiful too. There'd been a couple of men since Declan, besides Daniel, but Declan was the only one who'd ever made her feel special. Worshipped. Until that morning in London, when she'd learned he was returning to his ex. He probably hadn't given her a second thought since.

Yuki reclined on the banana lounge, letting the sun finish off drying her skin. It enveloped her in its rays, feeling like a warm, soothing bath. Or was it the heat of Declan's gaze on her body? Hard to say. She shook her head and spoke mostly to herself: "I haven't had a chance to swim in ages."

"Why is that? You're like a fish once you get started, or maybe a mermaid."

She glanced across at him, trying not to look too pleased at being compared to a mermaid. Daniel would have called her a child for such a thing. "Don't toy with me, Declan Moriarty. I know you only said that because I work for Mermaid Airlines."

"No, you are completely mistaken, my young Yuki. I think you're sleek as a seal but with pretty hair, is all."

She laughed despite herself. "I'm not so young. I'm nearly the same age now as you were when we met."

Declan raised an eyebrow and pretended to count on his fingers. "A mere babe, I was. But you still haven't told me why you've not been swimming for a while."

He was a babe. She didn't say it, of course. But he was smoking hot. More muscular than he had been six years ago and more secure in his tanned skin. Maybe that was what drew her to him—he seemed relaxed in his hotness, and he wasn't demanding anything, making her more comfortable around him.

Yuki rolled her neck from side to side, stretching out the last of her tension, and decided to give him the truth. "I haven't had much time for swimming or seeing sights when I travel. Life's been hectic with my ex-boyfriend. Always getting dressed up for some big event or travelling back and forth from Sydney and Singapore. He lives part of the time in Singapore, you know. But I don't have to worry about that anymore. He's got a new girlfriend." She hesitated because, actually, that woman was now his fiancée. "He's someone else's problem, I guess."

She hadn't thought of Daniel as a problem before. But that rang true. When she thought of him now, bells clanged in her head like a warning in hindsight.

Declan opened his mouth as if to speak but waited a few beats before saying, "Any man who'd cheat on you is soft in the head."

Yuki snapped her head around to look at him. "You can talk. What happened with your ex all those years ago? You went running back to her as soon as she called."

His face crumpled in on itself. "I did not. I went back to my job in Dublin. She just happened to be working there—until I could get her formally reprimanded, and she left for a direct competitor. You've probably heard how she tried to steal my business out from under me. I never thought... I didn't know what happened to you. I tried calling you and even went looking for you in London *and* Melbourne. You just disappeared, Yuki."

She swallowed hard, her throat suddenly too tight. Declan had looked for her? What did it mean? "I thought you and her—" Yuki shook her head. "She said on the phone that you were coming home to her. That you were getting married."

His face was a picture, now carefully blank. A muscle twitched at the corner of his jaw. "She called you? You actually spoke to her?" His voice was quiet, but full of controlled rage. It betrayed the emotions she'd thought she was alone in feeling.

Yuki shrugged, trying to keep her interest in this turn of events under wraps. "She called our hotel room in London when I was staying with you. She wanted to know who I was and what I was doing with 'her future husband'. I couldn't speak; I was so freaked out. And I didn't want to get into a big argument with you. You two had been together for a while. Obviously, it was serious."

"Serious as cancer." Declan stood, shaking out his hands as if washing them of the whole discussion. "She had no right to speak to you, not at all. I wasn't going back to her, and she knew that. I'd told her all about you, how I was falling so hard..."

She sat bolt upright in her lounge chair, hoicking up her bikini top as she went. It wouldn't be cool to have this discussion while experiencing a serious wardrobe malfunction. Declan seemed incapable of keeping his eyes off her boobs, in any case. His dark eyelashes flickered down, then up again.

She whispered, "You were saying?"

He blinked slowly. "God, Yuki. You must have known how I felt about you."

She stared up at him. "No, Declan. I'm not a mind reader. You could have said something. Anything! I talked to your ex, and she made me feel like the bitch 'other woman'. So I left before I did something completely stupid, like tell you I'd fallen in love with you." Yuki gasped and slapped her hands over her mouth, trying to take back her words.

Too late! Blabbermouth...

Declan's wide eyes were fixed on hers, and his lips. Those delicious lips parted as if he was in shock.

She lowered her hand from her mouth and placed her hands in her lap. She couldn't do this, not now. Declan was a constant pain in her heart, a wound that refused to heal. And nursing a fresh injury, she was currently raw as sushi. Her stupid ex had made her want to run away... and she'd run straight into Declan. It was raining ex-boyfriends. She stared down at her hands, her sparkly nail polish.

I could run away right now. No one could stop me.

Without saying another word, Yuki glanced at Declan, grabbed her towel, and fled in her flip-flops. The thwacking sound of her sandals striking the ground grew louder as she picked up speed, jogging across the courtyard. Completely ignoring him shouting her name, she didn't stop running until she reached the safety of her cabin.

After taking a micro-nap, Yuki headed down to the beach in her swimsuit, a floaty kaftan over the top. She strolled along the shoreline, stopping every few steps to collect shells. It was stunning down there, white sand and gorgeous azure water shining with the reflection of the sun.

She spotted some type of beach cabana, the sign attached to its roof marking it as an outdoor bar. Palm trees and lounge chairs surrounded the structure, but there were only a couple of people sitting there. Perfect. She could use a drink. As part of her relaxation project.

Yuki wandered up to the bar and indulged in some small talk with the handsome young Thai man pouring drinks. It turned out his name was Alfred, like Batman's butler. And like Batman's butler, he could apparently do magic. He whipped up a cocktail in a shaker while spinning and twirling the cocktail glass, then threw a little cherry in the air before popping it onto the rim of the glass.

She clapped her hands together. "Ooh, I'd love a piña colada. I've been dying for one ever since I arrived."

"No problem, Miss." Miss was much better than ma'am. And the way he smiled at her, his dark eyes shining, even had her grinning in return.

Again, Alfred worked his magic, finishing her cocktail just as the man who'd ordered the first one sauntered over to stand beside her. Declan, of course.

"Hello, Yuki. Of all the piña colada joints in all the towns in all the world..."

She grinned at him. "*Casablanca*. Nice. But how do you keep turning up wherever I am?"

He shrugged and leaned against the bamboo bar, all nonchalant. "Psychic powers. Or maybe I just wanted to hang out at the beach bar. Shall we sit?"

With a nod she picked up her drink, then headed over to a small round table with two wooden deck chairs.

Declan followed, close enough that Yuki could feel the heat of his body. Or that might have been her imagination, along with his spicy scent, which sent her mind hurtling back in time in an instant. Hot, slick skin, kissing, so much kissing, Declan, strong and muscular, holding her in her bed, under the pink quilt in the bedroom of her old apartment with silver stars stuck to the ceiling.

They'd met just before Christmas, and it was as if they were on a deadline to fit a whole relationship into a short time. It had almost worked out. For those few weeks after Christmas, they'd been happy. Okay, she'd been nervous about what was happening between them, but she'd been hopeful. Her future at that time seemed wide open, full of opportunity.

It was only later that she'd come crashing down to earth, not literally, thank goodness, as she was undertaking her flight attendant training. They'd been so wrapped up in each other during their time in London that the phone call from Declan's ex-girlfriend had left Yuki stunned. The whole situation had made it almost impossible for her to trust anyone since. She'd tried with Daniel. But that had got her nowhere.

Back in the here and now, she relaxed in her chair and sipped her drink. *Delicious.* Just like the man sitting opposite her. Yuki studied him, his blue eyes taking on a deeper cast the longer she held his gaze. Her attention dropped to his lips as he took a long sip of his drink.

"What are you playing at, Declan?" She popped her sunglasses back over her eyes to shade them from the glare. The sun gave everything a bleached-out effect.

Declan set his drink down and folded his arms over his impressively broad chest. His shirt was open a few buttons, so Yuki caught a glimpse of dark chest hair. She'd always liked that. He wasn't all buff and shiny like a gym junkie—he was more real, more old-school handsome.

He turned serious now, a crease forming in the space between his dark eyebrows. "I only want us to reconnect. I hope we can be friends, at least."

Yuki raised an eyebrow. "At least?"

His well-defined forearms resting on the table, Declan leaned forward. "Well, a starving man can always hope for a crumb of bread. Or cake if it's on offer."

She sputtered out a laugh. "Hoping for cake, are we? Well, I suppose there might be some wedding cake on offer this weekend."

"Not quite what I had in mind, Miss Yuki." He waggled his eyebrows at her, making her giggle.

It had been a while since she laughed properly, and Declan had managed to cheer her up within the space of just a few minutes. How did he do it? They'd spent time joking around, making each other laugh back in the day. And then there was their smouldering hotness in bed. She couldn't forget that. She hadn't experienced anything like it since.

Reconnecting with Declan could be fun. At some point. But now? Her head just wasn't in the game.

"I might consider cake in the future. But my menu needs to remain bland for now. Safe. Recent events have left me rather queasy."

"Understood." Declan nodded in the direction of the water. "Want to take a walk along the beach after our drinks?"

"That sounds nice."

They finished their cocktails and Yuki felt pleasantly buzzed. Whether it was the alcohol or the company, she couldn't say. In any case, when Declan took her hand and swung their linked hands between them, she gasped. His palm was hot and a little rough, enveloping her own hand. During their time together, she'd loved their size difference, his bulk and muscular presence making her feel small and delicate. She shivered. And it wasn't from the cold.

They walked along the beach together, the soft white sand deliciously warm beneath her bare feet, and Yuki couldn't remember the last time she'd felt so carefree and young. Declan definitely had an effect on her.

The question was, should she give in to chance and the opportunity to be with him again? Was the universe trying to tell her something? She should be sensible. It was too soon to decide, and right now, she needed a rest.

After walking for a few more minutes, she made her excuses and headed back to her cabin. She needed time to think.

As the cabin door closed behind her, Yuki breathed in the cool, scented air, perfumed with the jasmine votive candles in little holders in the bathroom. She'd take a bath. Properly relax. Or hide.

She grabbed a bottle of mineral water from the minibar. While taking a swig of cool water, she eyed the pills on the table nearby.

The doctor had given her a small supply of Valium, enough to last a few days. She'd said to take them only when needed, only if Yuki felt stressed or anxious. Well, the whole situation over the past few days had stressed her out. She popped two pills from the packet and swallowed them down with another gulp of water.

Yuki stripped off her swimsuit, feeling all her worries melt away. As she wandered through to the bathroom, taking the pills with her, the room appeared to shift and sway around her. It must have been the heat. The deep corner tub looked so inviting. She placed her meds on the counter and ran the warm water, watching ripples form tiny circles as she added a few drops of scented bath oil.

Once it was full enough, she grabbed her paperback romance novel and her bottle of water and placed both beside the tub. She sank into the water with a groan, relishing it as if immersing herself in a life-saving elixir. Which maybe it was. Because at that moment, Yuki didn't have a care in the world.

Declan knocked on the door of Yuki's cabin, louder this time. He couldn't understand why she wasn't answering. It had been a couple of hours, and he was a little worried. He understood, logically, that she was under no obligation to talk to him or spend time with him at all. But he wanted her to. And he was still concerned about her feeling ill.

He knocked on her door for the third time. Still no answer. Maybe she'd slipped out and he hadn't noticed. She might have gone somewhere with Sinead. With a shake of his head, he stepped away from her door and crossed the few metres to Gabriel and Sinead's suite—twice the size of his and Yuki's cabins. The pre-honeymooners had been locked in there for a while, but as soon as he got within earshot of their door, the moans he heard made him reconsider interrupting.

Sinead let out a high-pitched squeal, almost like the whistle of a teakettle boiling. Then the walls started to shake. The pre-wedding celebrations were going well then... Declan backed away and walked towards the hotel's reception instead.

When he strolled up to the desk, the young woman behind it beamed at him. Her shiny black hair swished as she gave him a nod. She was Thai, not Japanese-Australian, but she reminded him of Yuki. Not her looks, because she wasn't that similar to Yuki in truth. More that they were both working at hotel reception looking glamorous. Yuki's long, elegant neck and dark eyes had captivated him from the moment he first saw her, even before they started flirting.

Six years ago, Yuki had been working at reception when he'd attended an IT conference in Melbourne, Australia. He'd been bored out of his skull. The attraction had flared between them, hot and instant. They'd chatted, she'd laughed, and quite simply, she'd stolen his heart. He'd fallen for her before they'd even spent the night together.

"Sir, may I help you?"

He blinked at the receptionist's question. He'd been staring into space like an absolute muppet. "Ah, yes. My friend Miss Yamimoto isn't feeling well. She lost her phone just before we checked in. I was wondering if anyone had handed it in."

The young woman smiled at him, then shrugged in an offhand manner. "Let me see if there's a note about it." She tapped on her computer keyboard and obviously found something relevant because she glanced up at him with a look of confusion. "There was a phone found by a staff member but it's not in lost property. Let me find out what happened to it."

As she picked up the desk phone to make a call, Declan stepped back a pace and felt his own phone vibrate. He pulled it out of his back pocket to check. So far, he'd studiously ignored anything work-related, as they all knew he was on leave for three whole days. He had not been expecting a message from his mother back in Dublin, but there it was.

A brief flash of panic flared in his gut. Could something be wrong back home? Ma and Da weren't getting any younger... But no. His mother was in her usual fine form, sending him a meme from a TV series about murders on a tropical island, with a body washed up on a beach. *"Hope you're not dead, Son"* was the cheery caption.

Declan shook his head as he fought back a grin. All that meant was he owed her a phone call. His ma sometimes pretended to assume he was dead whenever he travelled and she hadn't heard from him for few days.

The receptionist hung up the phone with a click. "Sir, the phone is in the safe. But I'm sorry, but I can't release it to you. Your friend, Miss Yamimoto? She will need to come to reception herself."

Declan nodded, his thoughts now miles away, on his mother and her upcoming birthday. "Sure, I understand. Could you point me in the direction of a gift shop or a market? I want to buy my mother a gift. Perhaps Thai silk, something good quality."

The receptionist gave him directions to a nearby art gallery and a market. He was bound to find something to suit his mother from one of them. Maybe tomorrow he'd do some shopping before the wedding festivities began.

But first, he needed to see Yuki. He wanted to make sure she was well, obviously. Yuki may be willing to be friends. Or she might need a shoulder to cry on. Declan would gladly volunteer both shoulders for the job.

Chapter Six

Not Drowning, Waving

Yuki had barely managed to haul herself out of the tub; her head was spinning so oddly. Or it might have been the tub that was spinning. But who'd ever heard of a spinning tub? She'd somehow wrapped herself in a large plush towel and ended up sprawled on the enormous bed with deliciously soft covers. On top of the covers. Well, it was too hot for blankets.

She was just dozing off, falling into the start of a dream about warm, strong arms wrapped around her, a voice like whiskey in her ear, when she heard a knock at the door. Pounding, really. Her eyes popped open, staring straight at the ceiling fan, but the rest of her felt stuck to the bed by the weight of arms and legs coated in concrete.

"Yuki, are you in there?" The voice had that same warm, delicious tone as the one in her dream. "Yuki?" The door handle rattled.

Declan. That's who the voice belonged to. Well, he could come in. She'd missed him.

She coughed, trying to get her throat to remember how to speak. "Come in." Her voice sounded as if it came from deep underwater.

A chuckle like thunder rolled over her skin, raising goosebumps. "I can't come in, love. Your door's locked."

Oh. "Oh!" She sat up, the room rotated, and she almost lay back down. But she could do it. The door was only a few steps away...

Yuki rolled off the bed and landed on her knees with a huge crash. The force of the impact jarred her entire body, but she lurched forward into a crawl. Halfway across the hardwood floor, she had to stop to catch her breath and close her eyes for a second. Little stars danced behind her eyelids. The door handle rattled again.

"Yuki, should I call someone? Are you alright?"

Oh, right. Declan was here. He'd know what to do about concrete legs. He was smart. She inched forward like a caterpillar.

Before she knew it, she was at the door, flat on her stomach, waving one arm above her head, trying to reach the handle. When it didn't come any closer, she lurched up from all fours to grab the metal handle and yanked it down with a great tug. As she fell back onto all fours, the door cracked open, and a shard of piercing light hit her right between the eyes. It was like fireworks exploding in her brain.

She slapped a hand over her eyes. "Ow. Turn off the light."

"Oh God. Yuki?" The door clicked shut, and the fireworks faded.

Declan was suddenly there, crouched by her side, his thick thighs right beside her face. She lifted her head and rested her cheek on his leg. Surprisingly comfortable.

His hand stroked her hair, tangling in the lengths around her shoulders. "There now. What happened?"

"I-I fell off the bed. My head was all spinny."

"Okay, okay. I've got you. I'm going to lift you back onto the bed now."

Then Declan's arms were around her, just like in her dream. His big hands spread over the skin of her thighs, his fingers digging into her flesh as she flew up and over the side of the bed.

She landed with an *"oof"* as the air left her lungs and looked up to find Declan staring down at her with an odd expression. His face was slack, maybe in shock.

Yuki was pretty sure *she* must be in shock. She shivered as the overhead fan blew a fresh breeze across her skin, goosebumps prickling everywhere. She went to adjust the towel around her body, only to find it gone. With a gasp, she slapped one arm across her breasts and the other covering her bikini area. Too late—he'd seen the whole show. He'd seen it all before, of course, but that wasn't the point.

"Er, here's a blanket. You look a little cold." Declan tossed the cotton blanket from the end of the bed over her and roughly tucked it around her as if she were a toddler.

A flush of heat passed through her. "I can do that."

She tugged the blanket up, covering all the vital areas. The thing was, she wasn't embarrassed about being naked. She was embarrassed at being seen as incompetent or immature. Needing to be looked after. Okay, she was a *teensy* bit shy about being naked in front of this particular gorgeous man.

"Right. Of course." Declan sat on the edge of the bed, keeping his distance. "Can you tell me what happened now?"

His voice was kind. And the way he looked at her, carefully keeping his eyes on her face, made her heart expand and throb in her chest. "I took a bath, and I must have dozed off. When I woke up, I felt all woozy, and I had trouble getting into bed. My balance is off."

"You don't say?" His wry smile slid into concern again. "Can I feel your forehead? You might have a fever."

Yuki nodded, and then his warm hand was on her skin again, covering her brow. "You feel good to me. Perfect, in fact."

He cleared his throat and sat back again, watching her squirm. Because she was definitely squirming. His gentle touch had sent sparks of electricity shooting in all directions in her body.

Declan glanced around the room. "Is there anything I can get you? Water? Should I call the doctor again?"

With a sigh, Yuki settled more comfortably on the bed. "Water, please. I had some medicine earlier. Maybe that's what made me dizzy."

He frowned at her. "What medicine?"

"Just something to relax. I think I left it in the bathroom."

He nodded, scratching his chin. "I'll be right back."

Yuki watched his fine form leave the room, then got under the bedcovers and closed her eyes. She just needed a little rest.

"Yuki." Declan reached out to stroke her cheek. She looked so peaceful and innocent, sleeping like an angel. He could almost forget he'd just seen her naked. *Almost.*

Truth be told, his pulse still hadn't quite recovered its normal equilibrium. To be totally fair, he'd struggled for a long time to regain his equilibrium after he and Yuki parted ways. He'd missed her—more than he cared to admit. She was the one who got away.

"Yuki, can you hear me?" He stroked her cheek again, so smooth, so velvety. God, she was beautiful.

"Mmm." Her eyelashes fluttered open, but her eyes remained unfocused. "Hi, Declan. Did you say something?"

"Er, yes. I got you a glass of water. Try to keep your eyes open and sit up for me." She sat up, but in such a rush that she looked dizzy. The blanket slipped a good inch down her chest, nearly baring her sweet little nipples again.

Lord, give me strength... He sucked in a sharp breath and looked away for a moment. Yuki was stunning, but no way should he be touching her—or even thinking about touching her—in her present state. She could barely control her own limbs. However, it didn't stop him from being affected by her. He carefully adjusted how he sat, wanting to let a little more blood circulate below the belt area.

Declan picked up the glass of water from where he'd placed it on her bedside table. As he raised it in her direction, Yuki grasped the sheet and blanket and pulled it up to her chin. Yes. Good. All covered up and decent.

She took the glass from him with shaky hands and gulped down half of its contents in one go. "I didn't realise I was so sleepy. I drifted off in the tub."

He nodded. "I found your medicine. Valium. You took one after drinking alcohol?"

Yuki set the glass down on the bed beside her. It wobbled precariously. So did her chin. "I... took two pills. I forgot I had the piña colada. And the daiquiri." Her eyes filled with tears.

Declan reached out and stroked her cheek. "Ah hell. Don't cry. I wasn't sure you realised they shouldn't be combined. That Valium's extra strength too."

She smiled but it was an off-centre effort that made her look a little lost. "Yeah, I should have checked the milligrams." Her voice was deadpan serious, but he knew her too well.

That was a romantic comedy movie reference. He'd bet on it. "I know that one. *Working Girl.* Great film."

She bit her lip, holding back a laugh. "You know it?"

"Harrison Ford and Melanie Griffith, both in their prime. How could you go wrong?"

"Don't forget Sigourney Weaver in killer shoulder pads." She grinned at him, and it was like a ray of sunshine wrapped in a lightning bolt. Seriously, she had the ability to sear him from the inside out, like a reverse chargrilled steak. Or maybe he was just hungry.

Yuki was gazing at him like he held the moon and the stars in a trust account just for her. "There aren't many men who enjoy rom-com movies and openly admit it. I like that about you. A lot."

"I like *you*. I've missed you, Yuki."

She stared at him, an impassive look that had him worried he'd taken it too far. Not that he'd said much at all. Declan still feared her anger would rise again, like a coiled snake set to strike.

Yuki placed her glass on the bedside table and looked away. When she met his eyes again, it was a furtive glance before she studied her fingernails. She seemed nervous. "I like you too, Declan. I always have. But that doesn't mean I can instantly trust you."

He nodded and moved farther away from her. He perched on the edge of the bed, still a little too close to her gorgeous self.

She sighed and snuggled down under the bedding. "I suppose you should tell me what you've been up to. Apart from still being a handsome billionaire and all."

Declan stifled a laugh. "You know, I'm not really a billionaire. I sold off the majority of my IT and consulting businesses in the past couple of years and donated a lot of the proceeds to charity. I'm getting into the eco-resort business with Gabe, but that's just for fun. Soon I'll be mostly retired. Focusing on learning new things, trying to do something positive in the world." He grinned down at her confused face. "Still a handsome devil, though, it's true."

Yuki sputtered a little cough. "Well. I haven't read anything about that... I-I mean, I haven't heard what you were up to lately." She winced and covered her head with the sheet.

"I've kept a lot of information out of the press. But I'm interested that you've been keeping track of me." It wasn't a question. It was obvious that's what she'd meant.

She popped her head out from under the bedding. "Okay, yes. I've kept tabs on you. You're friends with Sinead and Gabriel. Why shouldn't I want to know what happened to you?"

Declan inclined his head to one side while trying to suppress a grin. "Aye, that's logical. A friend of a friend.

Except you're lying through your pretty teeth. You missed me too."

She blew out a gust of air. "Fine. I missed you a little bit. Tiny, really."

"I'm not so tiny."

"No, you're not." Yuki ran her gaze over his body, and his skin heated with the weight of her attention.

Declan stood, needing to escape this madness overtaking him. Because he wanted to kiss her. Not only that—he just wanted her. To push her down on the bed, lay his body over hers, and listen to her soft exhalations as she melted into him like she used to. He gazed down at her as he straightened up, running his fingers roughly over his hair.

"Don't go." Yuki reached for him.

He was powerless to resist her, of course. Declan could only do what she asked, could never do anything else. He took Yuki's hand and lay down beside her on the bed, deliberately on top of the sheets.

Declan ignored both the lump in his throat and the other rock-hard appendage that had caused him nothing but trouble over the years. He didn't want to scare her off, demanding things his body was ready for when, emotionally, they weren't even close. For once, he wouldn't be an arse, and he'd concentrate on putting his recent therapy to good use.

If he played his cards right, he might have another shot with Yuki. But first, he needed to look after her. And he needed a plan.

Chapter Seven

Good Morning

Yuki opened her eyes and shook her head, groaning at the residual images playing in her mind. Declan. Naked. The two of them tangled in her sheets. Flashes of his stormy-looking eyes gazing up at her from where he crouched between her thighs... It was just a dream.

She felt around with the hand of her arm flung across the bed but encountered only empty space beside her. No Declan, and no sign of him still in her room. He'd left rather than face her in the cold light of day.

"Right. Awesome."

Declan had been so big and warm in her bed last night, his hand casually holding hers, that she'd forgotten to wake up anxious. Instead, she was hyper-sensitive to every whisper of the sheets over her skin. And the gentle breeze drifting across her body made her want to run, naked, straight into Declan's arms.

Yuki sat up and stretched, planning out her strategy for the day. Now that she was up, she could tell the wedding day was starting out steamy. She'd been sweating. After unpeeling herself from the sheets, she took a quick shower and made herself semi-presentable.

She was due to meet Sinead in about an hour for the important bridesmaid task of preparing the bride for her big day. Not wanting to get dressed in her wedding outfit yet, she wrapped herself in the fluffy bathrobe hanging in the wardrobe and combed out her damp hair.

When she opened her blinds to take in the morning, palm trees waved above the roofs of nearby cabins, but the sky loomed dark and ominous. Was that a bad sign?

Yuki wasn't sure if Sinead had somehow angered the weather gods, but the stickiness and grey skies posed a potential problem. Her Spidey senses were tingling, warning of an impending storm. However, the wedding party would just have to suck it up. Her own dress was on the short side and cool enough, but Sinead planned to wear a full-length mermaid-style white gown covered with heavy beading and seed pearls.

An hour later, after consuming a coffee and all the complimentary cookies in her room, Yuki marched over to Sinead's cabin. Still wearing her bathrobe. Who cared if she looked like a disaster? She rapped on their cabin door, then, hearing nothing, clenched her right hand into a fist and banged. Hard.

"Just a minute," Sinead called out, her voice muffled.

"It's just me. I can come back," Yuki semi-shouted.

But just then, the door flew open, and a mess of blonde hair stuck through the doorway, attached to Sinead, clad in a bathrobe identical to her own.

Sinead grinned, her teeth flashing white behind an errant lock of hair. "Hi. Sorry, I um... overslept. Gabriel's just in the shower." She pushed the hair back from her face, and Yuki noted the pink glow suffusing her normally pale complexion. Her friend giggled. "Didn't get much sleep, to be honest."

Yuki giggled along with her, then stepped forward to speak, lowering her voice. "So, not going for tradition then? The groom was allowed to see you before the ceremony?"

"Oh, aye. He saw *everything*. I mean, um, we were just discussing wedding logistics."

Yuki nodded, folding her arms over her chest. "Uh-huh. Seriously, do you want me to come back later? There's still plenty of time to get you dressed and do your hair."

"Um, that might be a good idea. My sister, Bridie, is arriving from the airport soon. Maybe we could meet up in the breakfast room in a little while, if that's alright." Sinead nodded in the direction of the bathroom. "Gabriel and I still have a few more things to discuss."

Yuki shook her head as a wide grin stole across her friend's face. "I'm sure you do. Give him my love."

Sinead gave an exaggerated wink before closing the cabin door.

Now Yuki was at a loose end, with nothing to do before breakfast except maybe go back to bed. But then she had a better idea. The breeze picked up, making her shiver as she wandered back towards the far end of the swimming pool, past several cabins. One of them had to be Declan's.

She slowed her pace to check out the items left on the little porches outside the cabins. Kids' toys? Not Declan's room. A massive inflatable seahorse? No. A familiar pair of blue men's trainers lined up perfectly next to the door? Bingo.

Yuki approached his door with a churning stomach and a strong sense of déjà vu. She'd gone to his hotel room the first night they spent together, the week they'd met. It had been Christmas Eve. Sure, they'd had sensational sex, but that night had set off a series of events she didn't wish to revisit. But her mind spun through them anyway.

Losing her job. Gaining another, more challenging job where she'd had no clue what she was doing. Losing Declan. Moving to a new city where she knew no one. Feeling so lost, she ended up dating men who were totally wrong for her. And staying with one man for far too long, even when she knew in her heart it was over.

She had no interest in a repeat performance of any of those things when her life was already spinning out of control. Except maybe the sensational sex part. That could be fun. Her body heated until she was sweating again as she raised her hand and knocked on his door.

"Hang on, ya fecking tool!" The deep voice rang out from inside.

Yuki blinked a couple of times, and then the door swung open. A tanned, hairy chest appeared front and centre of her vision, and she honestly swooned. *God.* The man was built. She had to stop herself from reaching out to cling to his pecs. Instead, she laid a hand over her own heart and sucked in a breath. And remembered to lift her gaze to meet his eyes.

Declan stepped back a pace, his gaze flickering over her robe. "Er, sorry. I thought you were Gabe."

Yuki tilted her head to one side and examined him from head to toe. He looked good in his black boxer shorts and his naked everything else. She returned her attention to his face. "Do you usually talk to your friend like that?"

"Honestly, yeah. He calls me 'that Irish wanker', and that's how you know we're mates."

She raised an eyebrow. "Men are so weird."

"This is true." He hesitated, his mouth opening and closing again before his next words finally came out: "Do you want to come in?"

"Yes. I think we need to talk."

Declan groaned as she brushed past him, and she noted how his eyes dropped to her fluffy-robe-covered body as she passed. That was a good sign. It appeared he still wanted her.

She sat on the armchair beside his big, messy bed, inhaling the scent of him in the air. It was distracting. Yuki stared down at her pink-shimmer-painted fingernails, gathering her courage. "Okay. I was just thinking, there's no reason for us to act like strangers this weekend. I still like you; I think you like me, and we used to hook up. Maybe we could just... you know, hang out. Privately."

Declan was staring at her when she looked up. His eyes were so blue; if she wasn't careful, she could easily fall into them and drown. That was depressing. *No drowning*. Perhaps he hadn't grasped her meaning. Yuki's cheeks heated as the silence lengthened between them.

He cleared his throat. "Do you mean sleep together? Just for the weekend?"

"Maybe... I mean, *yes*." She thought back to a flustered Sinead grinning naughtily when she said she and Gabriel hadn't slept much. "But we don't have to do a lot of sleeping."

His confused expression was back, along with that crease between his eyebrows. Then if she wasn't mistaken, when she dropped her gaze for a second, his boxer shorts looked more form-fitting than earlier.

"Yuki, I..." He smoothed a hand over his tousled, gorgeously wavy hair. "I like you. Of course I do. But you've just been through a messy breakup."

She gave a shrug, deciding to put it out there. "I don't want to think about that right now. I just want to have some fun. And I'd like it to be with you. But I'm sure I could meet someone at the bar later if you're not interested—"

Declan cut through her words like a knife through butter. "Oh, I'm interested."

With that, he fell to his knees. Literally. It made Yuki suck in a sharp breath: it so closely mirrored the steamy dream that had woken her earlier. She caught his gaze as he looked up at her from in front of her knees, a cheeky grin lighting up his face.

"Let me show you how interested I am." His words came out on a deep rumble as his hands came to rest on her thighs.

Her legs began to tremble. "Please," she gasped.

It was Yuki's whispered *"Please"* that undid him.

Declan had placed his hands on her thighs merely to tease her. But he wasn't made of stone. Except for a certain part of his anatomy that currently resembled a slab of prefab concrete.

Interested. *That* was an understatement. He hadn't slept a wink, lying next to her last night, all warm and soft, so close to him that he'd almost exploded with want.

Now, he leaned into her warmth, bending over her smooth thighs, exposed by the bathrobe she wore. He pushed aside the towelling fabric and kissed each of her legs in turn.

Yuki let out a small, strangled sound before whispering again, "Please, Declan."

"You only had to ask." He smiled as he met her wide-eyed gaze, then focussed on the task before him.

Declan had planned to take things slow, but this would work too. Remind her of how good they were together, that he was here, now. Yuki had options, and he planned on making it impossible for her to ignore him.

He parted her knees with an insistent push, his thumbs firm on the tender flesh of the inside of each thigh. When he bent to kiss her legs again, he let his hands roam upwards, smoothing over her skin.

Yuki reclined in the armchair, and Declan couldn't help but sit back to admire the view. "Well, Miss Yuki. What a pretty picture you make."

He ran his hands further up the inside of her thighs, encouraging her to part her legs. She sighed, letting one of her hands come to rest on his shoulder as he bent forward again.

This time, he gave her no warning but dived straight between her legs and kissed her, the heart of her, like he'd kiss her mouth. He ran his tongue around her centre, tasting her, teasing her the way she liked. Yuki cried out, then hummed her pleasure as he set to work, circling his tongue.

Gripping her thighs, he proceeded to plunder her treasures like a damn pirate. He groaned at the little needy sounds she made while squirming beneath his touch. But he wouldn't let her go, wouldn't let her rest. Because he had to make her scream.

Declan had to give her what he'd been dreaming of ever since meeting her again: an orgasm to remember. A climax for the ages. He redoubled his efforts, losing himself in her scent, a floral concoction that made his head spin and his heart trip over its own beat.

Her legs shook under his grasp, and he knew she was close. So he gripped her thighs tighter as he counted down from one hundred in his head. He didn't want to lose control, not yet. This time, it was all about her.

"Declan! Oh my God..." He glanced up to find Yuki's head thrown back, her mouth open in a silent gasp as she teetered on the edge.

As his lips closed over her clit, Declan slid his right hand up her inner thigh. Finally, he was touching her most intimate place, his index finger sliding through her secret folds. He entered her with one finger, then thrust another inside before she could take a breath. She felt amazing. Soft and slick, her inner walls gripping him like she never wanted to let go.

Yuki screamed out his name, and he groaned at the way the sound reverberated against his lips as she clenched around his fingers. He kept sucking at her, moving his hand, wringing out the last waves of her climax.

Declan sensed her body relax before Yuki pulled away slightly. He kissed her intimately once more and gently removed his hand. Settled at her feet, he willed his body to relax as a heavy pulse beat in his chest and through his body.

Her gaze cleared as she looked down at him, blinking as if waking from a dream. Maybe she was dreaming, and he was a figment of her imagination. He'd certainly been in another reality for a while.

Yuki sat up straighter and adjusted the robe over her thighs. "Wow. That was... intense." She tilted her head downwards, watching him silently while he caught his breath. "Do you want me to...?"

Declan exhaled slowly, trying to regain his equilibrium. Somehow. "Er, no. I'll be grand. Aren't you due to meet up with Sinead soon?"

Her expression pinched into one of confusion. "But you're all... I don't want to leave you high and dry."

He shook his head. "I'll be fine. A cold shower's all I need."

"But why when we could—"

He let out another slow breath. "Look, have you ever heard of edging?" He shook his head as her frown deepened. "Good things come to those who wait."

Declan pushed off from the floor and steadied himself on the arm of the chair before standing tall. His erection was quite prominent in his boxers, it was true. When he risked another glance at Yuki's face, she was eyeing that general vicinity with a look of hunger that would have brought him to his knees a few years ago. Well, back to his knees.

He offered her his hand and helped her to her feet before leading her over to the door of his cabin. "I'll see you later. We have a wedding to organise, you know."

"Yes, but—"

Declan closed the door behind her before she could ask any more questions. Yes, a cold shower would be necessary. But all he really cared about was making sure Yuki wanted him more than she wanted her next breath.

So far, everything was going to plan.

When Yuki walked into the breakfast room a little later, she spotted Sinead sitting at a dark wooden table beside a planter box full of delicate white and purple orchids. Her friend waved to her and took a sip of coffee. Yuki straightened her little T-shirt dress and walked over to join her.

Yuki's head was still spinning after her interaction with Declan. He'd given her one of the most incredible orgasms of her life, left her floating on soft pink clouds, and then, while she was still seeing stars, backed off completely. Didn't even want her to touch him. She knew he was aroused, but it was as if he'd suddenly changed his mind and shooed her out of his cabin. What was that word he'd used? *Edging?* What did that even mean?

After taking a seat, she leaned over the table to kiss Sinead on the cheek.

"What's the matter, sweetie? You look all discombobulated." Her half-smile evaporated as she studied Yuki's face.

"Oh, um, I guess I am. Can I ask you a weird question?"

Sinead shrugged, her blonde ponytail slipping over her shoulder. "Of course."

"Do you know what *edging* is?"

Yuki raised an eyebrow as her friend burst out laughing and clutched at her chest, almost knocking over her glass of water. "I take it you're hanging out with Declan again. He's into all that New Age tantric stuff these days. Ever since he moved to Byron Bay and started seeing that hippie therapist."

Yuki had a moment of near meltdown at the thought of tantric sex with Declan. She shook it off and refocused on their conversation. "Oh. That's interesting. But what is it exactly?"

Sinead sat back, tilting her head, and waited a moment before answering. "Apparently, it's like delayed gratification. Holding off on an orgasm for a really long time, to make it more intense when it finally happens. You should talk to Declan about it. He'd probably explain it a lot better than me. Or maybe he could demonstrate!"

Yuki stared off into space, her thoughts whirling around in her head. Declan wanted to experience a super-intense orgasm with her? Well, that sounded awesome. There was no reason not to make his wish a reality. A wave of heat rolled through her body at the thought.

"Did you and he... spend some time together last night?" Sinead's question broke Yuki's trance. Her friend's half-smile was back, and she took another sip of her coffee while studying Yuki.

She nodded. "Yeah. And just between us, he gave me the most amazing orgasm this morning. But afterwards, he backed off completely and refused to let me return the favour."

Sinead sighed. "Ah. That sounds like Declan too. More than one woman has tried to get him out of his own head and to reach his heart. There was someone a couple of years ago who really hurt him. He hasn't fully got over it, if you ask me. It's almost as if he thinks he doesn't deserve love or happiness anymore."

Something sank in the depths of Yuki's stomach. "Oh. Poor Declan."

Yuki looked up as a waiter approached to take her order. Food seemed a good idea, but she opted for something simple: a Thai omelette, fresh fruit, and green tea. Her stomach was still unsettled after yesterday's nausea and the medicine she'd taken.

Her thoughts circled back to how well Declan had taken care of her when she'd been unwell yesterday. And in the morning, he'd anticipated her every desire. But before she could put her thoughts into words to discuss it with Sinead, a high-pitched squeal echoed through the room. Yuki whipped around to face the doorway.

"There she is! How's my beautiful sister?" A familiar redheaded woman in a green maxi dress dashed across the breakfast room and launched herself at Sinead. They embraced in a lopsided hug, Sinead staying seated, while laughing and gabbling to each other.

Yuki had met Bridie, Sinead's younger sister, a few times. She was wilder than Sinead and more impulsive, but her heart was in the right place. Bridie had helped to bridge the distance between Sinead and other members of their large family who'd been horrible to Sinead in the past.

Bridie looked well. She was more settled these days, not getting into so much trouble, or so Sinead had said.

Bridie took a seat close to her sister and immediately grabbed her coffee cup and drained it. "Hey, Yuki, great to see you."

Sinead picked up her cup and tipped it upside down to demonstrate that it was now empty. "Hey, get your own," she grumbled, but with a smile on her face. She plonked the cup back down. "Now that I have my two best girls here, I have something to tell you both."

Yuki flicked a glance at Bridie, who sat back in her chair and shrugged. Since Yuki was similarly clueless, she shook her head. When Yuki looked back at Sinead, she was positively bursting with excitement, bouncing up and down in her seat.

"Okay, brace positions. I'm pregnant! Not just with one baby, mind you, but two. I'm going to be a twin mumma!"

Bridie squealed and asked when Sinead was due.

"Oh, I'm only just three months gone. Plenty of time to organise my baby shower." Sinead grinned.

Bridie leaned in to hug her big sister again, whispering loud enough for Yuki to hear the words "Cool Auntie" and "best babies".

"Congratulations." Yuki smiled and then breathed out slowly. A tingle of excitement for her friend zipped through her body, followed by the sense that her own world was once again tipping from its proper axis.

Sinead was only a few years older than Yuki, but she was married to a handsome, wealthy man who adored her; plus, she had an education now and two beautiful houses, not to mention her own travel business. And soon, two children. While Yuki had... none of those things.

She was alone, still in the same job she'd had when Sinead showed her the ropes as a trainee flight attendant, and no closer to finding "The One". Daniel dumped her without warning, and now she had to start over in the relationship stakes. She pressed her hands down firmly on the table, trying not to grip the edge as if it were a life preserver.

After another deep breath, Yuki managed to give the appropriate response: "I'm so happy for you both, Sinead. Gabriel must be thrilled."

Sinead met her gaze now, tilting her head to one side the way she did when examining someone. She saw right through Yuki; that much was obvious. "Thanks. Gabriel *is* thrilled. He's a bit stressed out, you know how he is, but he's buying little baby clothes and even reading pregnancy books."

Bridie chuckled. "That's gold!" She then shot Yuki a kind-eyed look that said she also understood her current situation. Dumped, alone, completely adrift.

Sinead smiled at Yuki again and reached out to pat her arm. "I know you're having a hard time right now, but you'll be grand, I promise. Daniel was an arse, and you're well rid of him. And now you can be an honorary aunt to our twins. You're welcome to come stay with us as often as you like."

Yuki nodded and accepted the pot of tea set before her with a murmured word of thanks to the server. Sinead removed her hand, and Yuki poured her tea while Bridie ordered something involving mango slices, waffles, and Thai custard.

While sipping her tea, Yuki worked to identify the full range of emotions churning inside her. She'd thought she'd found everything she wanted with Daniel, early in their relationship. But she'd been wrong. So very wrong. She wasn't sure how long he'd been cheating and lying, but it had to be months, maybe even years. There was shame, humiliation, disappointment about a future never to be... but also a sense of freedom. She clung to that glimmer of positivity.

While she could hardly envision her life over the next few months, there was something to be said for a blank canvas. A fresh start. She smiled as their server returned with an omelette, cooked just the way she liked it. And as she took a bite of the most delicious thing she'd ever tasted, Yuki decided to focus on living in the moment.

Declan tracked down Gabriel, jogging along the beach. His friend loved to run, unlike Declan, who forced himself to because he knew it was good for managing his anxiety and his health in general.

Of course, the view here made it all worthwhile. The sun broke through the heavy clouds, casting a golden glow over palm trees and the white sand beach curving around into a cove. The sea sparkled: a wash of pale blues and greens that was as clear and fresh as the air.

"Hey, Gabe, wait up."

His friend was ahead of him, but Declan sprinted along the damp sand to catch up. Gabriel turned around and jogged backwards for a few steps before coming to a stop. "Well, if it isn't the Irish wanker."

Declan rolled his eyes as he caught up to his friend and slapped him on the back rather harder than necessary. "Well, if it isn't the old married dude."

With a muttered grumble about "Cheeky bastards", Gabriel turned and resumed jogging at a relaxed pace. Declan matched his stride, and they headed in the general direction of the beachfront bar.

After a moment, Gabe cleared his throat. "Mate, there's something I want to tell you. Ryan already knows, and Sinead's telling the girls today, but it's not general knowledge just yet."

He glanced at Gabriel, who wore a serious expression of concentration. Ryan was Gabriel's oldest friend and business partner, so he'd always tell him anything important, even if they didn't see each other often now that Ryan lived in London.

"Alright, out with it." He hoped Gabriel wasn't ill or anything. The man had already been through enough. Losing his mother to Alzheimer's at such a young age had been especially hard on his friend.

Gabriel nodded. "Okay. Sinead and I, well, we're going to be parents. We're expecting twins."

An exclamation mark screamed in Declan's head, and he came to a halt. "What did you say? Twins? Is she alright?"

Gabriel nodded, then leaned forward and rested his hands on his knees. "That's exactly how I reacted when Sinead told me. I thought she was ill, but it was just morning sickness. Man, I was so worried. But everything's great."

He stared at his friend. Gabe had it all: a successful business, a beautiful woman who appeared to be his soulmate, and now a family. While jealousy was not something Declan usually indulged in, there was a tinge of green at the edges of his vision.

After a second, Declan shook himself out of his mood. "Congratulations. You're a lucky man. Seriously, did you make a deal with a demon or something?"

His friend laughed as he straightened again. "Something like that. A few years ago, I promised to do everything in my power to make Sinead happy. And so far, it's working out great."

"I'd say so. Maybe I should try that. With Yuki, I mean."

Gabe turned to look at him, studying him until he felt like a bug under a microscope. His eyes widened at whatever he saw on Declan's face. "It's like that, is it? I always thought you two might get back together. She's a sweet girl."

Declan sucked in a deep breath and started jogging again. "She is. And I'm working on it."

Once his friend caught up and was jogging by his side again, Declan continued talking: "I stayed with her last night since she wasn't feeling well. She's like a magnet to me. I can't think straight when I'm around her. But I might have done something stupid."

"What happened?" Gabriel asked, his resigned tone saying he expected as much.

Declan shook his head again. He wasn't entirely sure what had happened. "I sort of pushed her away this morning. After she... well, we had a moment, but I panicked. She looked so perfect, and I fell under her spell for a while there. Yuki has a way of making me forget about anything else."

The pounding of his feet on the sand echoed his heartbeat as they jogged along. Finally, Gabe spoke: "Ryan once said something to me, like we're allowed to panic or have a mental blip, but it's important to let someone special know when they're loved. When they need reassurance, make sure that person understands you're there. Especially when it's an emotional time, or they're going through something difficult."

Declan nodded at the logic while quietly panicking again, but then he thought it through. He wouldn't have reacted like that—pushing her away before he could get her into bed—unless he really wanted Yuki. Unless he still loved her. He needed to talk to her. But by now, she'd be helping Sinead get ready for the wedding.

He'd talk to her right after the ceremony. They'd be plenty of time to work things out between them. And then he'd be sure to take her to bed and show her just how much he wanted her. That should work...

"Thanks, Gabe. You've actually helped."

"Don't sound so surprised," his friend grumbled under his breath, then took off at a hard run so Declan didn't have a hope of keeping up with him.

"We're all running our own race," Declan whispered.

His therapist's words were a comfort today. Declan wasn't out of time. He could choose his own path, and the way would open in front of him.

Chapter Eight

Here Comes the Bride

Yuki reached across the teak sideboard for the floral headpiece Sinead had ordered. She pinned it into the side of her hair while looking in the wall mirror. As one of Sinead's bridesmaids, Yuki wore a pale pink shift dress, and the matching pink orchids looked pretty against her black hair. Bridie, who stood close by, wore a silver dress, and her white and purple orchids stood out, brilliant against her copper-red hair.

They were getting ready in Sinead and Gabriel's cabin, a luxurious honeymoon suite, complete with a private garden and plunge pool. Sinead sat on the chaise lounge next to their king-sized bed, relaxing before she had to put on her dress. Now that Yuki knew Sinead was pregnant, she could see the signs: she was tired, needing a nap after lunch, and her stomach was gently curved in her silk slip.

"Just give me one more minute." Sinead closed her eyes and rested her head on a cushion.

They still had time, and they all looked gorgeous so far. At least, Yuki thought so. All their hairstyles were up-dos with loose waves around their faces, and their makeup was on point. The hair stylist who worked for the hotel and the local makeup artist were geniuses. Bridie offered Yuki a glass of champagne, and she happily accepted.

"I suspect my big sis might have stayed up too late last night." Bridie winked at Yuki before heading outside with her glass to sit in the sunshine.

The dark clouds had passed, for now. Yuki crossed her fingers, hoping the weather would hold. She followed Bridie and sat on a sun lounger, then took a sip of her drink.

"I saw the meme of you crying at that charity gala. Whoever posted it was a right arsehole." Bridie's words startled Yuki out of her thoughts.

Yuki had been staring at the pool, wondering if she'd have time for a swim later. No, probably not. "Oh. I guess everyone's seen it." She sighed and continued, "That was me at my worst moment. It hardly seems fair that's all the world knows about me."

"I know what you mean. Well, sort of. I had an embarrassing couple of years when I was younger and deep in debt, and it still follows me around. My reputation went to hell, and it's taken me a long time to find my feet again." Bridie sat back in her lounge chair and sipped her champagne. "I've also got a long hit list of terrible ex-boyfriends, so if you want to talk about it, I'm here."

Yuki nodded. She'd heard Sinead's version of events from a few years ago, about how Bridie had taken up with Sinead's abusive ex-boyfriend, Padraig, not knowing how twisted he was. Neither sister could be blamed for the way that loser stalked and threatened them. He was the one with problems, both legal and mental.

"I didn't know how to leave him." That wasn't what Yuki meant to say. But now it was out there, she realised it was true. "Daniel had me set up in his apartment in Sydney, and sometimes I went to his other place in Singapore while he was working there. I didn't have anything of my own. My family told me he was too controlling, but I couldn't see it at first. Sinead told me too. She said he reminded her of Padraig, and he'd only get worse over time."

Bridie made a humming sound of agreement. "I'm sorry."

Yuki set her glass down on a nearby table with a clink. "Daniel texted me just before my flight to Thailand. He ordered me to clear all my stuff out of the Sydney apartment by Monday. I don't even have a home to go to right now."

Bridie let out a loud sigh. "Men like that deserve a good flogging. You could stay with me if you like. I'm renting a two-bedroom place in South Melbourne, and my roommate moved out recently."

Something like excitement fluttered in Yuki's stomach. "Thanks for the offer. I'll definitely consider it."

She could stay with Bridie or someone else for a while. It wouldn't have to be forever. She could work out what she wanted to do longer term without crashing at Sinead and Gabriel's house during their second honeymoon phase.

A loud thump followed by a horrible hacking sound came from inside, making them both sit up straighter, and then Bridie leapt to her feet.

"Sinead?" She glanced at Yuki before hurrying over to the door and heading inside.

When Yuki followed a moment later, she found Bridie sitting beside Sinead on the lounge, holding her hand while Sinead threw up into a large plant pot.

"Oh no. Should I call Gabriel?" Yuki looked around wildly, searching for her phone. Which she still didn't have. Strange how she hadn't missed it. When social media was full of lies, staying connected to the world somehow lost its appeal.

Bridie glanced up and murmured, "Maybe you should go find him. I think he and Declan were meeting Ryan at the bar."

Yuki gave her a nod and, biting the inside of her lip, hurried outside. She'd forgotten to ask which bar the men were meeting at: the garden or the beach. Deciding to take her chances, she picked the bar adjoining the bistro and took off along the garden path, past the central swimming pool at a power-walking pace.

As she rounded the corner to the garden courtyard bar, clip-clopping in her heeled sandals and wishing she'd gone for flats, she spotted the three men standing by the long wooden bar with glasses of what looked like whiskey in hand. Ryan had arrived from London. His dark hair, neat beard, and imposing height made him stand out, along with his bright pink shirt. Gabriel leaned against a bar stool, facing away from her.

"Gabriel," she all but gasped as she skidded to a halt, seriously out of breath.

He turned to face her, his forehead creasing with obvious worry as soon as he met her gaze. He swiped a hand through the front of his dark blond hair, messing it up.

"What's wrong?" he asked in a gravelly voice just as Declan spoke her name.

She glanced at Declan long enough to appreciate the visual appeal of him dressed up in a grey linen suit and white shirt. But no time for ogling. She shot him a half-smile before flicking her attention back to Gabriel. "Sorry to bring bad news, but Sinead's sick. Bridie's with her, but she's really retching, and I don't know if she'll be ready for the ceremony in an hour."

Gabriel stared blankly at Yuki, then looked at Ryan. "Shit. I'm going. Let me make sure she's okay." Then he looked at Ryan. "What about the celebrant?"

Ryan shook his head. "Go, Gabe. Take care of her. Don't worry, I'll talk to the celebrant."

With a pat on the shoulder, Ryan sent Gabriel on his way, then whipped out his phone and had it pressed to his ear before Yuki could blink. As Ryan headed off towards the resort's main entrance, he gave them a wave while saying something about delaying the ceremony for a few hours.

As Gabriel jogged off towards the cabins, she called after him, "Do you want me to come with you?"

He shouted back, "No, you stay there. I'll call you later, Declan." And then he was gone, blocked from their view by a bamboo screen.

Yuki glanced at Declan, who shrugged and said, "Guess we'll have to find some way to entertain ourselves." He grinned, and it was the shiniest, most movie-starrish smile she'd ever seen. Oh, how she'd missed that shiny smile.

She folded her arms over her chest and sighed. "I hope Sinead's okay. Those babies seem to be taking a toll on her already."

Declan's gaze wandered over her body before he answered. Her skin turned to fire under his attention. "She's a strong woman; she'll be grand. Just like someone else I know."

With a shake of her head, Yuki blew out a breath. "Strong? Me? I hardly know whether I'm coming or going at the moment."

"More coming than going lately, I'd say." He waggled his eyebrows at her. Then his eyes raked over her again. As if he knew every inch of her body, which, to be fair, he did.

God, he'd make her explode again with a look like that. The blue of his eyes seemed deeper, more intense, as his gaze came to rest on her lips.

Her face burned with the heat of a thousand suns. Yes, he'd seen her come this morning. And now she couldn't stop thinking about it. How he'd touched her: as if he couldn't get enough, as if she was everything he needed.

Until he flipped a switch and instantly went from pulling her closer to pushing her away.

Yuki met Declan's eyes now and let her confusion show on her face. "I thought you'd changed your mind. That you didn't want me anymore."

His face fell into a half-angry, half-shocked expression that didn't suit him one bit. "That's not it at all."

He gestured to a bartender and pointed to his glass on the bar. A moment later, he had a fresh glass of whiskey. He downed it in one gulp, and Yuki tracked the movement of his throat, his Adam's apple bobbing. She wanted to kiss him there. To breathe him in.

Declan took a deep breath and put his glass back down on the bar with a thud. "I don't want to go any further unless we're both prepared to commit to something serious. I've been celibate for a long time, until this morning anyway. I'm not after some quick roll in the hay."

Yuki blinked several times, then simply stared at him. Celibate?

But what about...?

She stepped closer and whispered right beside his ear, "You weren't exactly celibate when you went down on me this morning. You were like a werewolf under the full moon, wanting to eat me alive."

Declan shivered, then took a step back. "Miss Yuki, I think we should go somewhere a little more private to discuss this further." His voice was all business, but his pupils had blown, and he stood like a soldier, his back ramrod straight.

Yuki wondered if something else was *ramrod straight*. Her eyes flicked downwards without waiting for her brain's permission. The impressive bulge in the front of his trousers confirmed her suspicions, and she glanced up at him with one eyebrow raised. He wanted her alright.

Declan cleared his throat and grabbed her hand.

Before she could fully register the warmth of his grasp, he shifted his grip so he circled her wrist with his thumb and forefinger, and Yuki found herself being pulled behind him. She clip-clopped across the floor, jogging after Declan as he marched along at an impressive pace.

When they reached the area by the pool, the wind had whipped up. Yuki pushed the loose strands of hair back from her face. This was the weather she'd been worried about earlier. A storm was brewing, and it had started sprinkling with rain. She tipped her head up to the sky for a second, enjoying the cool droplets against her skin. But then she remembered.

"Oh no, the wedding makeup! And my hair will be wrecked."

Declan glanced around and tugged on her arm again, pulling her into an alcove between a large suite and some type of gazebo. The space was a semi-indoor garden beneath a pergola, filled with orchids and other tropical hanging plants. Green and lush, like a jungle, it was decorated with dashes of wild colour, like something from a fantasy story. Immersed in the wonderland, she turned to ask Declan if he liked this place as much as she did. But her words evaporated in the steamy air.

With a groan, he pulled Yuki closer and enveloped her in his arms. His lips crashed down on hers, and she yelped before kissing him back urgently. His lips were soft and full, and she remembered him. Remembered this. The way he kissed was mind-melting.

Declan tasted her, devouring her with all the pent-up heat and energy he'd bottled up inside. His hands gripped her hips, squeezing as she wiggled against him. And when he finally broke the kiss, keeping their lower bodies still pressed together, she had to fight the impulse to launch herself at him and wrap her legs around his waist.

"Yuki." His voice came out low and partially strangled. She tilted her head back to keep her eyes locked with his. "You're so gorgeous it makes me lose my mind. I want you so badly it's messing with my concentration. But I need more than one night with you. I want us to give this thing between us another try."

Her pulse thrummed through her entire body, her hormones crying out for him to take her. Right here in the garden, she didn't care. She wanted to say yes to anything he asked, just because it might get the two of them naked, fast. But her head wasn't so sure. She'd been down this road before.

"Why have you been celibate?" Yuki hadn't meant to ask the question so directly, but out it popped anyway.

His forehead creased, even as his hand smoothed over the curve of her backside. "I've had a bad run of relationships, not even counting what happened with us. My last ex-girlfriend left me about two years ago after invading my privacy so viciously that I couldn't even believe it happened at first. She sold photos and information to the media. Stole money and things that were personal to me. I started therapy after a shitty time and a bad bout of depression. It was my therapist who suggested I stay away from relationships until I'd properly recovered. Until I met someone I could fully trust."

Wow. That's a lot.

Yuki's stomach flipped at the realisation he wanted her, for real. Trusted her. She reached up to plant a kiss on his jaw and nuzzled into his neck. The scent of him here was delicious and musky, mixed with the fresh citrus of after-shave. "I'm so sorry that happened to you. I feel burned by my ex. But it's still so recent. I don't know if I can commit to anything serious just yet. Even if I want to."

Declan pressed a kiss to the top of her head. "I understand, and I don't want to pressure you. I'll, er, let you get back to Sinead." He broke his hold on her and took a step back.

She reached for him, gripping his forearm. "No, wait. I don't want you to leave. What I meant to say is we should see how things go. Try being together for now. Then, in a while, we can discuss it like mature adults."

The creases reappeared on Declan's forehead before a shy smile tipped the corners of his mouth upwards. "So, Miss Yuki. You wouldn't mind if we rekindled our old flame?"

She peeked up at him from under her eyelashes. "You can rekindle my flame anytime."

He grinned, then licked his lower lip as he stepped towards her. "Your wish is my command."

With a rush of blood to his head and an urgency that made him feel like something feral, *like a wolf,* Declan closed the distance between them. He moved his hands to Yuki's hips and let himself feel the warmth of her beneath his palms. Let himself feel, full stop. His heart raced as he pressed his forehead against hers and simply breathed her in.

Yuki wrapped her arms around his neck, and it was like a dance. Like the night they'd first slept together after dancing underneath the stars on Christmas Eve years ago. Although they'd only shared a few weeks together back then, he'd never once regretted his time with Yuki. His only regret was not letting her know how hard he'd fallen for her.

But he'd not make that mistake again. He had time. *They* had time.

Leaning down, he pressed his lips to hers. She opened to him, her tongue tangling with his. Yuki bit his lower lip, teasing him into a dizzying state of arousal he'd normally push back with an iron fist. But not today. Declan wanted to feel all that she did to him.

His hands found her arse, its rounded contours fitting into his hands even better than years ago. He squeezed her flesh through her little pink dress, and Yuki gasped against his lips. Pulling her closer, he pressed his rock-hard erection into her stomach. And almost blacked out.

"My God, I want you." He groaned out the words as she inched a hand between their bodies and palmed him through his trousers.

Yuki nodded against his neck. "I can tell. Is this all for me? Please say yes."

Declan let out a long breath. "Yes. But not yet."

Her grunt of frustration had him chuckling under his breath, despite the fact he could scarcely breathe.

"When?" she squeaked out.

He pulled her closer still, until she ground herself against him. "Tonight. After the wedding. We'll go back to my room. And we'll have all night." Declan could wait. He'd waited so long already. An eternity.

But first... Declan ducked his head and kissed down Yuki's throat, letting his hands roam lower at the same time. Her dress was made of some sort of stretchy fabric, so it was easy to ruck it up higher, over her thighs. Easy to expose her lace underwear. So easy to move them aside to make way for his questing fingers. And slipping his fingers through her slickness was the easiest thing in the world.

As his fingertips ghosted over her tight bud, Yuki moaned. "Fuck, Declan!"

He chuckled, enjoying the chance to see her let go. He continued his exploration, circling and stroking, and within minutes, she was rocking against him. Using two fingers, he entered her in a single, smooth thrust. Then she was clenching, giving herself up for him.

Yuki grasped the front of his shirt—her hands tightened into fists—until slowly, she came back down to earth. As Declan watched, her dazed expression cleared, and the sweetest smile crossed her face.

"Wow. Flame officially rekindled." She pressed a chaste kiss to his cheek.

"Mmm." He hadn't had any relief, of course. Declan still burned for her, still wanted her with every inch of his being. But he would wait because she was worth it.

He squeezed her waist and stepped back from her warmth and temptation. "Right, gorgeous girl. We'd better go see how the bride and groom are getting on."

Yuki straightened her underwear and he helped to smooth down her dress, trying not to get carried away and undress her fully. Later, he wanted her naked, both of them bare. With a giggle, she watched as he adjusted himself.

His expression must have been quite the picture. He grimaced as he turned to face her. "Laugh at your peril, Miss Yuki. I have plans for you later."

Her eyes were comically wide as they left the garden together, holding hands.

Chapter Nine

Wedding: Take Two

By the time Yuki knocked on Sinead's door, she'd tidied herself up and fixed her lipstick. But she hadn't recovered from the second climax Declan had given her in one day. The man was a revelation. Her cheeks were warm, probably still glowing pink, and her body felt loose and languid.

Bridie opened the door and stuck her head outside. She stared at Yuki and offered a cheeky grin. "Hello, so you've decided to join us, have you? Did Declan need a nap?"

Yuki's face burned red-hot, and she ducked her head as she entered the room. "We were just getting reacquainted. How's Sinead?" A few steps inside, and she could see for herself.

Her friend looked a thousand times better than she had earlier. She was seated at the room's small dining table, eating pancakes and drinking tea.

Sinead tipped her head at Yuki and waved her fork in greeting. "I'm grand now. Gabriel just went to talk to Ryan and the celebrant. We're getting married at five o'clock."

"Oh, that's good. Was it just morning sickness?" Yuki walked over to stand by the table while Bridie settled on the sofa and took a sip of her own tea.

"Hmm, more like all-day sickness. I've been much better the last week or so, but it hit me hard today. It comes in waves and then settles again. Now, sit down and tell me all about you and Declan."

Yuki took a seat, ducking her head to avoid Sinead's direct gaze. She didn't know why she was embarrassed. She'd always discussed her love life with her friend in the past.

I don't want to jinx it. Because Declan is special. He always was.

Distracted by her random thoughts, she didn't register Sinead's next words at first. But they slowly filtered through to her still orgasm-hazy brain. "You look like you've been hit right in the feels. Did you shag him then? He's one sexy fella, if you ask me."

"What? I... not exactly. But he's definitely sexy." She huffed out a breath and watched as Sinead popped another forkful of pancake into her mouth. "Declan wants us to be together again. To try a proper relationship."

Bridie piped up from the sofa. "Well, that's good, isn't it? He's nice, a good-looking man, smart too. He knows what he wants. And it seems like he wants *you*."

Yuki nodded, absently thinking about the man who'd recently dumped her. "But Daniel said he wanted me too. He promised we'd get married. And look what happened there."

As the two sisters locked gazes, Yuki flicked her attention between them. Wearing identical frowns, they exchanged some kind of wordless communication before turning back to stare at her, silence echoing through the room.

Yuki sat back in her seat and crossed her arms. "What?"

Sinead smoothed a few loose strands of her hair with her fingers as she asked quietly, "Did he ever promise you that, though? Or did you just wish it were so?" She reached across the table and placed a hand over Yuki's. "I'd been trying to get you to tell me what was going on with you and Daniel for months. He was leading you a merry dance between Sydney and Singapore and wherever else. When was the last time you even stayed together for more than a couple of days?"

A lump formed in Yuki's throat, and the room grew suddenly too hot. She grabbed Sinead's glass of water and took a gulp before placing it back down on the table. The ice cubes danced and swirled around the slice of lime. "Six months, maybe longer. I'd have to check my calendar. He said it was a busy time at work. He had so many new plastic surgery clients, and he had to attend conferences. I was alone a lot. Left behind."

With a sigh, Sinead glanced across at her sister again. She turned back and patted Yuki's hand. "Daniel let you go a long time ago, and now you need to let him go too. He wasn't kind, and you don't owe him a damned thing."

Bridie rose from her seat and came over to sit beside Yuki. "My big sister's right. That ex of yours sounds like an absolute arse. Declan, on the other hand... well, he's a fine man. If you're not interested, I might even give him my number."

"I know, right? If I didn't have Gabriel, I'd be happy for Declan to keep me warm at night." Sinead winked, then hooted out a laugh as Yuki snatched her hand from her grasp.

Yuki banged her hand down on the table. "He's not up for grabs, girls. He wants me, and I want him. I might even be a teensy bit in love. That's all that matters."

Sinead grinned at her while Bridie's shoulders shook with silent laughter. Yuki knew she'd been out-manoeuvred by the Kennealy sisters, tricked into admitting her true feelings, but she didn't care. As happiness overtook her, she relaxed and allowed herself to feel it—from the top of her head to the tips of her toes and everywhere in between, especially her heart.

A teensy bit in love. Well, wasn't that something?

Declan had met up with the other guys to get ready for the ceremony in Ryan's fancy suite. He stood in front of the wall mirror, re-tying his tie for the third time. But his concentration was *shite*. All he could think about was Yuki and those soft little sounds as he touched her. He threw his tie on the floor in frustration.

Gabriel stood across the room, having just emerged from the bathroom. Declan noted he now looked respectable after his second go at getting dressed. His summer suit was stylish and his shirt open at the collar. He'd ditched his tie.

"Hey, Gabe. Why do I have to wear a damned tie if you don't?" Declan grumbled.

His friend shrugged. "You don't. I just didn't want you looking like a complete dog's breakfast."

Declan slapped a hand against his leg. "Gah! Arsehole. You know I hate suits and ties."

Ryan sat in an armchair and snorted, rolling up the sleeves of his bold silver shirt. At least he'd changed from the hideous pink one. "Not everyone's capable of achieving my level of sartorial elegance. Gabe needed to impose *some* standards."

Declan turned to glare at him. "Look fella, you wear pink shirts that looks like Barbie's cast-offs. And you're Australian. Not a nation known for its fashion. Except for budgie smugglers."

Gabriel piped up: "I'll have you know I rock a pair of Speedos. Anyway, I'm sure Yuki will be happy with whatever you wear." He raised an eyebrow at Declan in a challenge.

For a moment, Declan's brain short-circuited, and he stood perfectly still. He nodded slowly. "Aye, Yuki's a wonderful woman. But she prefers my shirt off as a general rule."

The other two men laughed but soon fell silent when Declan let out a long, calming breath and closed his eyes.

Thoughts of Yuki made him unsteady. He hoped they were on the same page, but he was far from certain.

Gabriel asked, "Mate, are you okay?" His concern was evident in his careful tone.

Declan blinked his eyes open. "I will be, I think. Yuki and I have decided to give it another go. But you know how gun-shy I am when it comes to relationships these days."

With a quick glance at Ryan, Gabe walked over to stand in front of Declan. "That's understandable. You've had some bad experiences, but that doesn't mean you should miss out on this chance. You like her, right?"

Beneath his ribs, Declan's heart thudded out of rhythm. *Like*. Such a weak word for the feelings Yuki inspired. "It's entirely possible I more than *like* her."

Gabe put a hand on his shoulder and met Declan's gaze. "You deserve a good relationship with someone who cares about you. Yuki could be the one, so it's worth a shot."

"Alright, guys, enough with all this emotional crap. We have a second wedding show to get on the road." Ryan rose from his seat as both Declan and Gabriel stared at him. "What? Touchy-feely moment done and dusted. Let's move it along."

Gabriel sighed. "He has the emotional maturity of a wet rag. But don't let him put you off. He's mooning around, waiting for a phone call from his old *friend* Charlotte."

"Am not." Ryan crossed his arms with a scowl.

"How old are you, nine?" Gabe shook his head and turned back to Declan. "If you want my advice, don't let Yuki leave this resort before discussing how you feel. I made that mistake with Sinead when we first met, and I almost lost her."

Declan clenched his jaw and made a pact with himself. "I'll make sure Yuki understands how I feel." He only hoped he didn't scare her off.

In Sinead's suite, the girls were getting ready for the ceremony. Yuki, who'd been hanging on to a surprise gift for Sinead, bounced on her toes as she dropped the blue crystal pin into her friend's waiting hand. "Here. This is for you. Something blue."

Sinead gasped as she took a closer look at the delicate piece of jewellery. "Oh, a little mermaid. Thank you! I love it."

The long end of the pin was in the shape of a mermaid tail, with alternating crystals representing scales, and the mermaid's long hair was picked out in thin swirls of silver. Yuki helped pin it into her friend's hair, where it was swept up on one side. She grinned. It looked perfect.

"Oh, let me see." Bridie hurried over from the other side of the room to examine Sinead's hair. "That's gorgeous. Now it's time for my gift." She rummaged around in the beige bag hanging over the back of her chair. "Here we are. Something old."

Bridie placed something in her sister's hand and squeezed their palms together. When she pulled her hand away, a stunning string of creamy white pearls lay in Sinead's palm. "They were Gran's. I might have claimed them when we were teenagers. They're yours now."

Sinead held them up against her throat and studied herself in the mirror. She still wore a bathrobe, but she suddenly looked glamorous. "Oh, my heart. I missed out on all of this the first time around. Eloping seemed so romantic, but I missed all these traditions."

Yuki pressed her lips together, trying to shake off the unexpected wave of sadness that passed over her. She was happy for her friend, honestly. Maybe they were partly happy tears. Yuki turned away and took a deep breath.

It was almost time for the ceremony. They needed to get Sinead into her dress. Yuki grabbed the garment bag from the wardrobe where it hung and unzipped it. There it was, like something out of her own dreams. Yes, she wanted to get married. Someday.

Okay, she'd wanted to marry Daniel. But he'd always said there was no rush—they were still young; why get married when they didn't even have a home yet? Except they both got older, he bought the Sydney apartment, and it was still never the right time. Now she realised he'd been busy leaving her behind.

Don't think about it.

But she couldn't help thinking about it. A few months ago, she'd gone to lunch with Daniel and some of his friends, and Yuki had drunk a little too much champagne. One thing led to another, and later she'd proposed to Daniel in bed. He hadn't said a word in response. He'd just got out of bed and left, flying off to Hong Kong to attend a conference. Had he considered her feelings at all? His blank expression still haunted her. A knot of anxiety formed in her belly. Maybe he'd really broken up with her that day.

"Oh, that dress is gorgeous." Bridie's words interrupted Yuki's unpleasant memories.

Then Sinead came to stand by her side, Bridie on the other, and Yuki had no time for sadness. This was a happy occasion for Sinead, and she'd do anything for her friend.

Yuki unzipped the dress, and using Bridie's arm to steady herself, Sinead stepped into it. Its silk lining skimmed over her body, the ivory colour perfectly complementing her pale Irish skin tone. Yuki zipped up the side seam while Sinead straightened the shoulder straps, and Bridie held up the beaded skirts.

A moment later, they stepped back to admire Sinead. She looked like she'd stepped out of the pages of a bridal magazine.

Yuki smoothed the loose ends of Sinead's hair behind her shoulders and sighed. "There. Now you're perfect." There was a touch of awe in her voice.

"Almost. I just need a handsome groom. Hmm, I wonder where I might find one?" Sinead grinned at them, and the three women dissolved into fits of giggles.

Yuki decided she'd be happy, at least for today. If she could believe it, she could be it.

Declan cast a sideways glance at Gabe, who stood on his right-hand side. His friend looked nervous. Which, for a man who'd already been married for several years, who had a beautiful wife who clearly loved him and a family already underway, seemed sort of ridiculous. And sweet. Because Gabe wanted to make Sinead happy above all else. If she wanted a second wedding, she got it.

They stood on the beach, at the end of an aisle of white silk carpet, under an arbour decorated with tropical flowers. It was a beautiful setting, sure. However, the dark clouds looming overhead threatened rain. Declan tipped his head up and shaded his eyes against the glare. The sun was half out, making the steel-blue ocean sparkle. Maybe they'd get the ceremony done before the storm arrived.

Ryan stood to Declan's left, the ring safely stored in his jacket pocket. He was taking his best man duties seriously, making sure Gabriel had a stiff drink.

Gabe took a slug of whiskey from Ryan's flask and handed it back. "I hope the girls are on time," he muttered under his breath.

As thunder rumbled in the distance, the men all looked at each other, Gabriel's brow furrowing with worry, and then Declan glanced in the direction of the resort. The celebrant, an older woman in a white suit, stood at a short distance away waiting with a couple of staff members.

The women were about to make their entrance from the resort through a nearby gazebo draped with white curtains. One of the hotel staff hit the music, a small sound system rigged to the gazebo hosting the speakers, and the hypnotic sound of Nick Cave's "Into My Arms" set the mood.

Bridie appeared first, marching ahead of the other two women in a silver dress, her head held high as the wind whipped her red hair around her face, just as the first fat drops of rain fell. She cast a suspicious glance at the sky before marching on.

Yuki stepped from the gazebo next, and Declan was mesmerised. Her body moved with a fluidity he'd always admired, that little pink dress clinging to her curves for dear life. She held a posy of pink and white flowers in front of her, and he couldn't help but imagine a different setting.

In his mind's eye, the beach dissolved, and in its place stood the old stone church near his parents' house in Ireland. Yuki would be dressed in pure white silk, a long train trailing behind her as she passed wooden pews filled with her family on one side of the aisle. On his side, his parents would be sitting up front, plus old friends and an assortment of cousins. His own little sister Caitlin would be a bridesmaid, along with Sinead, in a reversal of today's roles. When Yuki eventually became his bride.

Declan shook himself out of his daydream as Bridie walked up to stand nearby and Yuki drew nearer, walking down the white carpet towards him. When Yuki stood a few paces away, she locked eyes with him and smiled a sweet, secret smile, her dark eyes alight with mischief. He turned to watch the sway of her hips as she passed by.

Then Sinead caught his attention out of the corner of his eye. She looked stunning, as always, but to him, she still wasn't a patch on the woman who'd captured the whole of his interest and, quite possibly, his heart. Sinead grinned at Gabe as she walked towards him, the drops of rain falling on her hair and flowers only making her prettier.

By the time he'd returned his attention to Gabriel, the rain was falling harder. As a hotel staffer named Chris flitted around, snapping photos, the celebrant began to speak. But it was all a blur to Declan as he stood opposite Yuki.

She smiled at him again, her full lips rosy with a shiny gloss he longed to lick from them. It was as if the world had a shimmer to it despite the wind and rain making their presence known.

Declan refocused on the celebrant as she asked, "Gabriel, will you continue to have Sinead as your partner, your love, your wife, and your other half in the union of marriage, for as long as you both shall live?"

"I will." Gabriel's answer was clear and unequivocal, his voice hoarse with emotion.

Declan glanced between Gabriel's and Sinead's faces, aglow with the type of adoration he'd always chased. They were a pair—they'd do anything for each other. When he returned his attention to Yuki, he spied tears welling in her eyes before she blinked them away.

When it was Sinead's turn to answer whether she would continue to keep Gabriel as her husband, she lit up with a wide smile and replied, "Of course I will. I always will."

She giggled as Gabriel pulled her close, and, with fingers entwined, they stared into each other's eyes.

After giving them a moment, Ryan cleared his throat to interrupt and passed Gabe a small box from his pocket.

Sinead laughed again as Gabe tried to slide a new eternity ring onto her finger. He jiggled and removed it and tried once more but to no avail.

"Sorry, my fingers are swollen at the moment. Here, put it on my necklace." Sinead turned and offered the back of her neck to Gabriel, who undid the clasp and threaded the ring over the string of pearls. After reclosing the clasp, he kissed the nape of her neck.

Declan chanced a look at Yuki, who he found already watching him. Her face was flushed a gorgeous shade of pink, and her eyes still sparkled. Her gaze flickered over his body, and his skin heated as if her eyes held a lick of flame.

Another roll of thunder was enough to get the celebrant hurrying through the remainder of the ceremony—a short blessing—until all that was left was a kiss to seal the deal.

Of course, every fairytale needs a villain, or so Declan had always been told. It seemed the happy couple had somehow displeased the gods. Or perhaps it was a watery blessing from above. In either case, when Gabriel bent to kiss Sinead and wrapped her in his arms, the heavens opened.

Sinead and Bridie both screamed as the deluge struck, rain so heavy they had no hope of reaching cover before getting completely soaked. But they ran, with Sinead pulling Gabe along by the hand. Ryan jogged along behind them with his jacket over his head.

Declan looked around and laughed, and although the sound was barely audible above the rumble of thunder and the *whoosh* of rain, he felt the laughter inside, echoing in his chest. He held out his arm to Yuki, and she clung to him as they made a dash for it back towards the resort. Together.

Chapter Ten

After The Storm

Yuki uncrossed her legs and squeezed them tight under the table in the resort's private dining room, willing her resolve to be strong enough to last a tiny bit longer. Unfortunately, seated beside her, Declan looked just as edible as the platters of Thai delicacies on the bridal party's table. His jaw was shadowed with dark stubble that would leave marks on her throat, her thighs...

Later.

Declan glanced at her with eyes that danced with desire. He might have been befuddled by hormones. Her ability to form sentences had fled and her brain turned to sludge the second Declan nudged her foot with his under the table. Now, the lengths of their thighs touched through their clothes.

Yuki had wanted him so badly after the ceremony, when they were drenched and his white shirt clung to every contour of his chest, like a modern-day Mr Darcy who'd been dunked in a lake. But Sinead had called out for Yuki to follow her and help her change, and she'd been with their group ever since. It had been fun hanging with the girls, but she was impatient to get Declan alone.

The bridal party was currently discussing ideal travel destinations. Gabriel had claimed to love trekking in the mountains of South America, and Sinead was openly mocking him for nearly fainting from heatstroke at Machu Picchu. Yuki grinned at her friend across the table.

"I hope you're enjoying your dinner," Declan whispered close to Yuki's ear.

Tingles ran down her spine at his nearness and the soft gust of his breath against her neck. "Oh, I am. This garlic chicken's delicious. But I hope I don't have garlic breath later."

"I'll take my chances. Perhaps you need some dessert?"

Yuki met his eyes, and yes, that was definitely desire. The heat in his gaze was enough to sear the skin clean off her bones. She wanted her clothes gone, the two of them pressed together, sharing body heat. No matter that it was a steamy night in the tropics.

"Maybe I should have an early night. I'm kind of tired." She pressed her lips together to keep from giggling.

Declan leaned back and shrugged, feigning nonchalance. "Sure, I could walk you back to your room." His hand came to rest on her knee, and Yuki let out a long exhale to slow her rapid breathing.

Yuki looked up to see Sinead watching her, a small smile playing on her lips. Her friend mouthed the word "Go."

Not needing to be told twice, she rose from the table, and Declan stood beside her, making excuses about jet lag and the time difference catching up with him. She doubted anyone was buying what he was selling, but she didn't care.

When Yuki caught Bridie's eye, the other girl winked before raising her glass in a mock toast. Ryan simply tipped his chin in their direction, saying goodnight without words. Gabriel raised an eyebrow and nudged Sinead before whispering something to his wife.

Yuki said goodnight, and the group replied as one. Spirits were high, and maybe a few saucy jokes were murmured at their expense, but that didn't matter to her. She and Declan made their way out of the room, grinning at each other every few seconds.

And then they were outside. Walking beneath the palm trees. Her hand in his. Running in high heels, the breeze fresh against her flushed cheeks, her hair whipping across her face. Declan squeezed her hand, and she was the happiest she could remember in almost forever.

Declan tugged Yuki close on the steps of her cabin. As her body pressed against his, her arms wound around his neck, and there was no better feeling in the world than when their lips met. She let out a little sound, and he swallowed it, tasting her sweetness as she opened up to him. He was already hard, so hard, and wanting everything, all of her, all at once.

Yuki pulled back and grinned up at him. "Come on."

Seconds passed as she fumbled for her key in her clutch purse. Then they tumbled inside and closed the door behind them so they could continue kissing in privacy.

Declan pressed her up against the wooden door, and their kiss became incendiary. As the fire built within his belly, he tilted his head to kiss down her neck, and the way she gasped had him wondering if she was just as on edge as he was. But no, that was impossible.

It had been two long years since he'd been with a woman, and the thought of breaking that drought, of being inside her, almost had him exploding before they even got naked. He had to make this good, had to convince Yuki they were meant to be together, always.

Yuki hooked a leg around his thigh, and he took the hint, lifting her and wrapping both of her legs behind his back. Her dress hitched up her thighs, and he grasped her bare skin as he kissed her deeper, then groaned as she rocked against him.

Declan ducked his head to kiss a path along her low neckline, the softness of her skin there and the scent of roses driving him mad. "Right, I think we should move this to the bedroom," he murmured against her skin.

Yuki nodded before whispering, "It's all one room except the bathroom."

"You know what I mean."

"Yes." She pressed a kiss to his jaw.

He carried her across the room to the bed, pausing only to let her kick off her shoes, then set her down on her back on the white sheets. Wanting to take a moment to appreciate her, he drew back and stood before her to enjoy the visual feast.

Yuki looked deliciously rumpled, her long dark hair spread around her head like a halo, pink lip gloss smudged, and her dress hitched up almost to her waist, revealing silver lace underwear between her legs. That sight had him groaning again, and he palmed himself through his trousers, squeezing to keep himself in check.

She sat up, staring at him, watching his hand. "I can do that. Let me." The words fell from her lips like a benediction. She wanted this.

Declan exhaled roughly and ran a hand through his hair, which had flopped in front of his eyes. Yuki leaned forward and tugged him by the belt, undoing it before he could say a word. She pushed his trousers and boxers down to mid-thigh, then her hands were on him, and her grasp on his straining erection was enough to make his eyes roll back in his head.

"Condom? Now?" she asked, gazing up at him. Seeing her like that, on her knees on the edge of the bed, touching him, stroking him, almost gave him an embolism.

"Wait." He cleared his throat and placed a firm hand over hers. "I won't last long if you keep doing that."

"Oh. But I like it. Declan, you're beautiful." She leaned forward to kiss the swollen tip, and he stumbled back on jelly legs.

"Condom. Where?" he managed to croak out.

Yuki grinned. "Bedside table. Here, I'll get it." She turned and crawled across the bed, and he marvelled in the sight of her arse, round and perfect, still encased in her figure-hugging dress.

While she rummaged in the drawer, Declan ripped his shirt off over his head, removed his shoes and got rid of his trousers and boxers completely.

Then she was back in front of him, opening the foil packet and sheathing him in a perfect, fluid stroke that had him cursing. It was too good. His pulse pounded in his head. "Christ, sweetheart. You'll be the death of me."

Yuki smiled—a cheeky expression that tightened his chest. "I hope not. You have a job to do. You need to keep me warm. I'm a bit cold. Might take off my dress."

That made zero sense, but he stared as she undid her side zipper and dragged her dress off over her head. Clad only a translucent silver bra and those skimpy matching knickers, she blew his mind.

As heat surged to his groin, he grew impossibly hard, robbing his head of blood. He refocused, concentrating on the ugly painting of a sailing ship on the wall for a count of three so he didn't black out.

"Declan, are you with me?" A laugh was captured in her voice.

He shook his head to clear it. "God, yes." Declan climbed onto the bed and hovered above her, leaning on his forearms. He lowered his head to suck her tight little nipples through the lace of her bra.

Yuki bucked her hips with a gasp. "Don't make me wait any longer."

Declan was in full agreement. They'd waited long enough. While inching her underwear down, he kissed his way across her breasts and tugged the edge of her bra down with his teeth. Sucking her sweet flesh, he groaned when, a second later, she squirmed. Then her knickers were gone. Somehow, she also managed to undo the clasp of her bra behind her back.

With Yuki lying naked beneath him, he lowered himself and rested more of his weight on her body. The feel of it, their bodies pressing fully together, had them both gasping.

Declan licked and teased her nipples, circling with his tongue until the little peaks tightened and she cried out. She wrapped her legs around his waist and said the words he'd longed to hear: "I want you, Declan. Now."

"Yes, my love." He kissed her lips as he touched her, stroking her, aligning their bodies.

When he entered her, the heat of her body shocked him to the core. He surged forward, her slickness easing the way. He hadn't meant to go so fast, but he was seated inside her in one smooth motion, leaning over her, watching her dark eyes widen as she squeezed around him.

"Declan, oh, you're so deep." Yuki gasped again as he shifted his weight, and she wrapped her legs around him.

Declan gritted his teeth. She felt too perfect. It was too much. He flexed his hips and began to move. Grabbing a handful of her arse, he pulled her towards him, groaning as she followed his lead and rolled her hips.

He wouldn't last much longer... couldn't hold on...

Yuki grasped his shoulders and squeezed, her body tensing and then shuddering.

"Oh God!" She cried out and screwed her eyes shut.

As she tightened around him, Declan was lost. A shower of lights sparked behind his closed eyelids. A shimmer of gold. Thrusting into her heat with an urgency he couldn't deny, he let go and rode out the waves of his climax.

When he came back to reality, he lay sprawled on top of Yuki, his face pressed to her throat. He kissed her there, then remembered something he'd said to her without thinking, in the moment.

"Are you alright?" he asked gently, hoping she didn't think him a complete embarrassment. He'd struggled to make it good, worried he'd finished too quickly.

"Mmm," she hummed against his shoulder. "You were always gorgeous. Now I suspect I'm addicted."

Declan kissed her neck, just under her ear. "Addicted?"

"Addicted to you. To us."

Well, that had to be the best news he'd heard all year. For several years, in fact. "Ah, Yuki. My beautiful girl. I'm addicted to you too."

She nodded against his shoulder. "I know. You said you love me."

Declan stilled. He'd said that, no denying it. He lifted his head to look her in the eye, and what he saw made him relax somewhat. Yuki seemed... content.

She snaked an arm between them and pressed her palm over his heart. "It's okay. I think I'm in love with you too."

After that, there was nothing to do but take her in the shower. Then the bed again. And show her exactly how much he loved her. Adored her. Later, he let her take him, and Yuki rode him like she'd never get enough.

They had all night. And it was just the beginning.

Morning arrived with a crash of cymbals and flashing lights in her brain. Okay, that wasn't quite the case. But someone was banging around in Yuki's room, making a hell of a racket.

Declan. Last night. They'd slept together... well, not that there'd been much sleeping.

Mmm. What a delicious man.

Yuki opened one eye. Why was every light on, making her eyeballs burn? She sat up slowly, clutching the sheet to her front while pushing her hair out of her eyes. Once she'd adjusted to the brightness, she realised the windows had been thrown open, letting in a burst of golden sunshine along with a fresh sea breeze. Declan stood in the tiny kitchenette, busy with the coffeemaker.

"Morning, Miss Yuki. Can I interest you in a croissant and coffee?" He'd turned to face her, his smile as white and movie-star-shiny as it had been when they first met.

Her stomach flipped, and not just because she was hungry. She grinned at him, probably blushed too. Her face sure felt hot. The things he'd done to her... Well, it was sensational. "Oh, yes, please."

Declan sauntered towards the bed, a tray balanced on one hand like an expert. In his other hand, he held flowers: purple orchids like the ones in the resort's gardens. He set the tray beside her on the bed and placed the orchids in her outstretched hand. When he leaned in to kiss her, she sighed with satisfaction.

"Voilà, one breakfast. Sorry I woke you, but I wasn't sure if you were flying out today." Declan shrugged, then sat on the edge of the bed, down near her knees.

Yuki stilled, her hand frozen on the coffee cup. "I was meant to fly back to Sydney this afternoon, but now I'm not so sure. My ex wants me out of the apartment, but I don't even want to go get my stuff yet. I don't want to see him."

Gently stroking her knee through the sheet, Declan replied, "You should come home with me. I have a house in Byron Bay now with plenty of space. You can have your own room. No pressure."

Noting the tense set of his jaw, Yuki knew this was important to Declan. She also knew he was a kind man who might not actually want her to move in with him. He probably just felt sorry for her. "Is it okay if I think about it? I can change my flight later if I need to." She took a sip of coffee. Its heat soaked into her bones and warmed her; the thought of seeing her ex again had chilled her to the bone.

Declan nodded, his gaze focussing intently on her face. "Of course, sweetheart. I'm sure you could stay here for a couple more days if you want. Sinead said she booked their suite until Wednesday."

"I'm not too sure about hanging out with the re-newly-weds until then. But it's an option. Bridie said I could stay with her in Melbourne too. That's also a possibility."

She studied the scruff on his jaw, wanting to rub herself up against it like a cat. But she needed to be sensible. They were having a grown-up conversation; jumping his bones again would be entirely inappropriate.

He raised an eyebrow at her. "You don't sound sure. What do you want to do?"

Yuki sighed. "Honestly, I don't know. I'm due back at work on Tuesday, but even so... I don't think I'm ready. I have a ton of leave days I haven't used, and I think I need more time off to think."

Declan nodded again, then stood and turned away from her. He walked over to the window and leaned on the frame with one elbow while looking out. "Some time off is a good idea. And I forgot to tell you, someone found your phone yesterday. They're holding it for you at reception. Apparently, only you can collect it."

From his body language, she could tell he was tense. It was strange, especially given how relaxed he'd been last night after they'd thoroughly debauched each other. "Oh, it's turned up? That's good. I'll go grab it after breakfast."

Yuki took a bite of her croissant and groaned at how perfect the pastry was. Flaky, buttery, and delicious. When she glanced up at Declan, he was staring at her mouth. Maybe he wasn't completely immune to her charms this morning.

She licked her lips. "You could always come back to bed. There's no reason for us to be up yet."

Declan sighed and walked over to her again. After kissing her on the top of her head, he murmured, "Actually, I have to go. My flight leaves this afternoon, and I still need to pack and speak to Gabe about work. But call me as soon as you know what your plans are. Okay?"

Yuki looked up, his forehead was creased in apparent concern. "Oh. Okay."

He stroked his fingers through her hair and caught her gaze. "Ah, Yuki, I want to be clear with you. I want us to be together, to have more of what we shared last night. But I don't want to force you to decide immediately when you're going through a tough time. So, if I don't hear from you in the next few days, I'll check in with Sinead or Bridie. I can come and get you anytime."

Why was he talking as if she were about to fall off the face of the earth? She was trying to figure out which way to go. She had some stuff to sort out. That was normal, right?

Yuki reached out to grab the back of Declan's neck and pulled him down for a kiss. She most likely had horrible morning breath, but she needed this. He kissed her back gently, so carefully. She pulled away a moment later, still wanting more. But Declan didn't appear to be on the same wavelength.

"I'll see you soon," he said. Then he turned and walked out of her cabin before she had a chance to say goodbye.

While finishing her croissant, Yuki tried to figure out what it all meant. Wherever she decided to stay, she could still make a go of it with Declan. Couldn't she?

When Declan walked into the breakfast room, he found Gabe sitting alone. Perfect. He wanted to run something past him before talking to Yuki or Sinead.

Since waking at five o'clock, his head had been spinning with plans for the future, but he couldn't trust his own instincts when business and love were combined. His prior relationship disasters were a testament to that.

Don't beat yourself up. It takes two to tango. Or ruin a relationship.

His therapist's voice was loud in his head this morning. That he'd called her in the early hours and left a voicemail might have had something to do with his current mood. He didn't want to push his luck with Yuki. If he tried to pressure her into a relationship, he might end up pushing her away.

As he approached Gabe's table, his friend smiled, the corners of his eyes crinkling up in the way they did when he was relaxed. "Good morning. Have a good night?"

Declan sat and drummed his fingertips on the table. "Yes. Not exactly...I mean, yes. But now I'm stressed."

Gabe stared at him for a moment before saying, "Okay. Out with it."

Declan exhaled slowly. "I'm in love with Yuki."

His friend shrugged and then topped up his cup from the small ceramic teapot on his table. "I guessed as much. You could hardly keep your eyes off her yesterday. What happened? Did you two...? Wait, was it bad?"

"Oh, things are fine in that department. Better than fine. Mind-blowing, in fact."

Gabe grinned. "So, what's the problem?"

Declan spoke fast, letting all the thoughts spinning around in his head come tumbling out. "I want her to move in with me. I've already asked her. And I want to marry her. I have my grandmother's ring, and I can picture the dress she'd wear. A wedding in Ireland. Then kids. I think we should have three, but we'd need to discuss it. But she needs a man who won't disappoint her, and what if I do? What if I can't give her what she deserves? But I don't think my heart can take it if she turns me down. So maybe I should back off."

"Woah, slow down, mate. You've got yourself in a right mental tangle, I can see that. But let's take one thing at a time." He paused and eyed Declan, his expression serious. "You love her. Does she love you?"

With a quick nod, Declan said, "Aye, I think so."

"Good. Excellent. But moving in with you. That's pretty fast. I take it she's told you about her ex kicking her out? The guy's a real dickhead, no doubt about it."

Declan leaned forward, placing his phone on the table. "Have you seen social media? That guy's all over it, telling everyone how Yuki was just a silly young girl, holding him back. Apparently, now he's moved on and found true love with his heiress. They're going on some big reality TV wedding show. He claims Yuki was cheating on him. It's dire."

"Oh shit. No, I haven't seen it. Not sure I want to. I'll talk to Sinead. We need to make sure Yuki's protected if the media come after her."

"Thanks, mate. I knew you'd get it. And there's something else. I want to organise a new job for Yuki, just in case. If she goes back to work as a flight attendant, there'll be no hiding from public scrutiny. I was thinking,

Sinead's travel agency needs some more experienced travel and tours staff. People who speak different languages."

Gabe leaned back in his chair now, nodding thoughtfully. "Right. Good idea. Sinead can see if she's interested. I'd prefer if she was really into it before we offer her anything formally."

Drumming his fingers on the table again, Declan tried to relax and sort through the worries in his head. "Good. I think that's everything. I'll head home and make sure I'm ready if Yuki wants to come and stay with me. But I won't force it. It has to be her choice."

"Of course. Try to relax. We've all got her back, and yours too."

When Declan left the resort, he needed to know he had a plan in place. It wasn't the plan he'd have chosen. He'd wanted to suggest dating, getting to know each other better, maybe going somewhere quiet for another weekend away.

Now he understood Yuki would be under fire from all directions. She didn't need anyone else putting pressure on her. Declan would let her come to him, or not at all. As much as it would kill him, he'd let her go if that's what she needed.

Yuki had showered, dressed, put on fresh makeup, and was feeling as good as anyone could on only a few hours of sleep. However, when she entered the hotel reception, she couldn't help but notice that the staff fell suddenly silent. Did she have something on her clothes? Spinach in her teeth? No, she hadn't even eaten any. She glanced down at her outfit—neat shirt and pants—and couldn't see anything wrong.

There was the woman in a black uniform behind the reception desk, someone she hadn't seen before, who'd gone suspiciously quiet. The porter hauling a cart of luggage stopped and stared, and even the gardener, who held a watering can in one hand, flooded a poor potted palm while gaping at her.

She approached the reception desk with growing unease. Something was wrong. "Um, hello. I believe someone found my phone. I'm Yuki Yamimoto."

"Oh, of course you are. Just one moment." The receptionist looked flustered, her eyes shifting sideways while she spoke and her cheeks flushing a rosy pink. Of course, Yuki's probably were too, given that everyone was staring at her.

What on earth is happening?

While Yuki waited for the receptionist to return from the back office, a creepy-crawly sense that someone else was watching her prickled at the back of her neck. As she turned to face the open doors and the resort's circular driveway outside, something moving in the trees to the left captured her attention. A whirring, clicking sound, then... *Crash!* Someone fell out of a palm tree beside the doors and landed on the concrete.

Yuki stepped forward to see if they were okay but was halted by a firm grip on her elbow.

"Don't go out there," said a man by her side. She turned to find the porter, a young man with short black hair and a serious expression, watching the situation outside.

"What's going on?" She craned her neck to see.

A security guard was out there now, hauling a man to his feet. The man who'd fallen from a tree. He didn't look like a local: his Hawaiian shirt and camera bag, coupled with his scraggly ginger hair and beard, marked him as a tourist. Yuki had a sense she'd seen him around before.

The porter spoke low in her ear. "I think it's best you return to your cabin, Miss Yamimoto."

As she glanced at him, she could feel her pinched "what the hell?" expression. No doubt her confusion was showing.

"He is a photographer, Miss. We are having some trouble with the media today. Please." He held out an arm to usher her towards the resort's indoor walkway, which led back to the swimming pool area.

Yuki stopped long enough to grab her phone from the receptionist, whose wide, dark eyes regarded her with apparent trepidation. What was wrong? Was she in some kind of trouble?

She thanked the woman for her phone and stuffed it in her pants pocket. Then she power-walked back to her cabin as fast as she could manage.

Yuki settled on her freshly made bed and stretched out her legs. She plugged in her phone, which had gone dead. All the different notifications scrolling down the screen as she restarted it had her frowning again. Hundreds of people had messaged her. There were emails too—including one from her supervisor at Mermaid Airlines. She tackled that first.

Apparently, she now had an extra week of paid leave and an appointment at the Melbourne office next week to discuss her "personal situation". Again, *what on earth?* She emailed back quickly to confirm her attendance, without knowing anything more.

Her Instagram notifications had blown up too. Usually, she posted a few selfies and food photos when travelling, but she hadn't even had time to take any snaps this trip. Then she read some of the messages:

He's so hot I can't believe you cheated on him!
Low rent behaviour
Gross! Ur ugly anyway
You slag
What makes you think you're good enough for Daniel you cow?

There were lots of messages in Japanese and Mandarin too.

Oh, shitballs.

It was all about Daniel, her bloody ex. Of course, it was. What had he done now? She opened her browser and searched her own name, and immediately wished she hadn't.

The images on multiple magazine sites and social media channels made her gasp. It was her in those photos—she was sure of it, even if they were all grainy like they'd been taken from a distance. And it was Declan with her. Kissing her. Lifting her dress in the resort's garden. Touching her.

Then there were other pics of her by the pool in her yellow bikini, pulling up her bra top like she'd just been naked, and, of course, they'd caught her expression. She was staring at Declan, as if undressing him with her eyes.

Sinead featured too, on the beach in her wedding dress, and Yuki and Declan in their wedding outfits, holding hands, running together in the rain. Sinead's private wedding—splashed across the media. God, her friend would probably be angry too. Hopefully Sinead wouldn't blame her for the invasion of privacy.

When she searched Daniel's name, her face grew even hotter, and she swore at the screen. He'd sold some bullshit story about Yuki and their relationship imploding to a Singaporean magazine and was plugging some reality TVS show he was appearing on. With the heiress. His new fiancée. Who was apparently already five months pregnant. He claimed Yuki had constantly cheated on him and had taken off on vacation with all his credit cards. Oh, and apparently Yuki was trying to steal his apartment out from under him.

With tears pooling in her eyes, she sucked in a deep breath and searched for Declan's phone number. Despite blocking him, she had it saved from years ago, but was it still the right number? She hit the call button and held the phone to her ear.

He answered. "Yuki? Are you alright?"

Even though he couldn't see her, she still shook her head. "No. I'm not. Can you come here? Please?"

Her voice shook as she told him she'd seen some photos online...

"I'll be right there, sweetheart."

His voice was gravelly and so gorgeous; she pressed her hand to her heart as it thudded under her breasts. She closed her eyes. And waited.

As soon as Yuki opened the door, Declan threw his arms around her and shuffled them both inside her cabin. He closed the door behind them before kissing her cheek and wiping away her tears with his thumb.

She gazed up at him with watery eyes like reflecting pools. "You came."

"Of course." He kissed her lips, just a gentle peck to let her know he cared.

"I was so worried you'd hate me. This is just like your ex-girlfriend. The media... the lies."

Declan nodded as he clenched his jaw. Yes, those memories were still fresh enough. But it was his ex who'd caused that whole disaster; she'd brought him nothing but a pile of shit on top of all the pain. Not Yuki. His beautiful girl was a light at the end of the long tunnel he'd been staring down for years.

So, some arsehole had taken photos of them together and sold them to the media. No prizes for guessing who was responsible. Yuki's ex-boyfriend seemed like a true publicity whore.

He lifted her chin until she met his gaze. "No. This isn't your fault. I would've preferred our privacy, but it is what it is. Now, what can I do to help?"

"Will you hold me?"

"Yes, my love."

She sounded as sad as he'd ever heard her, and that tore at his heart. Yuki was usually made up of bubbles and light, so this trembling, shadow of herself wasn't right. He led her to the bed, and they lay down, her back against his chest. Big spoon to her little spoon, he wrapped her in his arms and held her close.

Declan stroked his fingers through Yuki's hair, and finally she relaxed, the tension melting from her body. And he relaxed against her, enjoying the chance to be with her, quiet and safe.

Sometime later, a groggy Declan blinked his eyes open. Someone was banging on the door. He snuck from the bed so as not to disturb Yuki and tiptoed to the door. When he eased it open just a crack, Gabriel and Bridie stood outside. With a frown, he opened the door a little wider.

"What's going on?" His gaze ping-ponged between the two of them.

Gabe spoke quietly, as if wanting to keep a secret: "I've organised a private jet to take Bridie and Yuki straight to Melbourne. Yuki can stay at Bridie's place for a while. No one knows Bridie, so she won't be followed. Apparently, there's a large media contingent at the airport terminal in Bangkok, but we'll fly them out of a smaller airstrip."

"Hell. This is like something out of a spy movie. You really think Yuki needs a safe house?"

Gabriel sighed. "I do, unfortunately. My security guy in Melbourne will keep an eye on Bridie's apartment. You know what can happen when the paparazzi gets busy, even if it's a beat-up story."

Bridie placed a hand on Gabe's arm and nodded at Declan. "Is Yuki asleep?"

"Not anymore." Yuki came up behind Declan and peered around him at the visitors. "I'll go with you, Bridie. It's a good idea. There's nothing I'll need from the Sydney apartment in the next few days."

She avoided calling the apartment home, Declan noted. He clenched his jaw and stuffed his hands in his pockets. He really wanted Yuki to come to his house and stay with him for as long as she wished. But it was a selfish impulse. Thanks to his ex-girlfriend, certain segments of the media knew where his Byron Bay house was located.

Declan turned to Yuki and stroked a thumb across her cheekbone. "Of course. I'll let you pack." With a quick peck on her cheek, he headed out the door to talk to Gabe.

Bridie went inside with Yuki, who waved at him with a half-smile on her face before closing the cabin door.

With a long, slow exhalation, Declan reminded himself to breathe. To be in the moment. Everything would work out for the best. He only wished he truly believed that.

No more than an hour later, Yuki followed Bridie out the resort's side entrance to a waiting limo. Once her suitcase was stowed in the back, there was nothing left to do other than say goodbye to Sinead, who'd come to see them off. Her friend hugged Bridie and they said their goodbyes. Yuki heard Bridie promise to keep Sinead updated on any trouble.

Declan hadn't reappeared, but he'd texted to say he didn't want to cause a fuss. Whatever that meant. Yuki enjoyed fuss, generally speaking. She wanted the dramatic movie-style goodbye kiss, although she was sure she'd see

Declan again soon. Pretty sure. Like, seventy-eight per cent.

Yuki held her phone in her hand, but it felt more like a grenade. She just wanted to be rid of it. She didn't want to see any more social media notifications, and all her other messages could wait.

As if she'd conjured him with her thoughts, a familiar little fellow appeared from the tree line and ran right up to her on the concrete path beside the driveway. A monkey. Could it be the same one who'd stolen her phone the other day? She suspected so. There was something about the way he stared up at her, his head tilted to one side... eyeing up her phone.

Yuki huffed out a laugh that was half exasperation. "Are you looking for this? My phone?" she asked the little guy, who responded with a grunt that sounded like agreement.

She glanced over her shoulder at Sinead and Bridie, watching on in obvious disbelief.

Bridie snapped a photo on her phone. "This is just for you, not for socials!"

Yuki nodded as she crouched in front of the monkey. "Okay, here's the deal. I no longer want this. You can have it." She held out her right hand, the phone resting on her outstretched palm.

The monkey grabbed it from her, and a second later, he was off back into the trees, most likely texting all his little monkey mates.

"I'm ready to go now," she announced as she straightened and smiled at Bridie.

Then they were off too, seated inside a limo with tinted windows. Yuki hoped she was doing the right thing. It felt an awful lot like leaving Declan, or so the sick feeling in her stomach told her.

Chapter Eleven

Hideout

Melbourne, Australia

Yuki was bouncing off the walls, with nothing to do at Bridie's place except eat, sleep, and watch movies on her streaming accounts. She'd done all of that and now was bored out of her mind. The past few days, Yuki had stayed indoors while Bridie went off to work at an advertising agency in the city as usual. Bridie, who was a social media manager, had a few good tips for her about the whole ridiculous situation.

Bridie's number one tip was to go private mode on every social media platform or simply close her accounts and to say nothing. She'd explained, *"You don't want to feed the beast"*. Yuki had obviously ditched her old phone, so she'd closed the account and bought a new phone with a new number. She'd saved her contacts but all her socials were deactivated. She'd gone old-school and was lying low. Bridie had told her not to even call anyone yet, and so far, Yuki had been good. But now, she wanted to be naughty.

Her fingers itched to call Declan. Seated on the cushy emerald-green loveseat near the windows of Bridie's apartment, she flung aside the new Talia Hibbert book she'd been trying to read. The love story wasn't grabbing her like usual, and she knew it was because her head was spinning with thoughts of Declan. Thoughts of the future.

Her meeting with Mermaid Airlines yesterday had been a wake-up call. Yuki didn't want to go back to being a flight attendant. They'd offered to put her on different routes to avoid certain parts of Asia, but she no longer wanted to be in the public eye. According to Bridie, people as far away as London and New York were commenting on her ex-boyfriend's stupid made-up stories.

Yuki picked up her phone from the coffee table and searched for Declan's number, wanting to message him before she could talk herself out of it.

Yuki: Hey Declan, it's me. Yuki. I have a new phone number!

Yuki: Just wanted to tell you I'm okay. Staying with Bridie is fine but boring... She works a lot.

Declan: Calling you right now.

Yuki answered his call and let out a long sigh.

"Hello, beautiful." His voice was low and gravelly, like it was after he'd kissed her. When they'd been in bed together.

A wave of heat rolled through her lower belly. "Declan. I've missed you so much."

"Me too, love. Tell me, when are you coming to stay with me?"

She pressed her lips together to stop a bubble of laughter from escaping. Declan still wanted her. Thank goodness. "You really want me to come?"

A deep chuckle vibrated against her ear. "I always want you to come, darlin'. Come to me now, and I promise I'll make that my mission in life."

Yuki giggled, sitting up straighter in excitement. "Really? I mean, you don't mind me coming to live with you?"

"It's my dearest wish. And you're my dearest girl."

She grinned. "Oh, Declan. You're the best. I want to kiss you."

"Mmm. I'll kiss you soon enough. I'll book you a flight to Byron and meet you at the airport. Let's put the booking under the name Mrs Moriarty, just to be safe."

She laughed again, sure that Declan loved calling her his wife, even if it was fake. For now. "Can't wait to see you. I love you."

"And I love you too. Now, go get ready. I'll text you with the flight details soon."

Yuki couldn't help making kissing sounds at him before ending the call. That made him laugh. She was so happy she could burst.

She danced around Bridie's living room, picking up her things to throw in her suitcase. There wasn't much to pack, and soon she'd be with Declan again.

Yuki crossed her fingers and wished with all her might that everything would work out for the best. She had a good feeling that this was what she was meant to do.

Ballina Byron Gateway Airport, Australia

Three hours later, Declan stood waiting by the arrivals gate at Ballina's regional airport, sweating in his chinos and white shirt. He'd rushed to be there on time for Yuki's flight, which he'd been lucky to book on such short notice. The priority ticket was a favour from a friend who worked for the airline.

Declan was ridiculously nervous. Even though she'd said she loved him, even though he believed her, and even though he knew in his heart they were meant to be together, he'd had love or the universe laugh at him too many times to take anything for granted. It was hard to believe he wasn't cursed.

When her flight landed and the passengers came streaming through the gate, he held his breath. Then, there she was. Her shiny black hair sparkled under the bright lighting, and her little pink and white dress clung in all the right places. But it was her dazzling smile that punched the breath from his lungs. They locked eyes, and the world melted away, fuzzy at the edges, like the best sort of dream.

All he could see was the object of his desires, the keeper of his every wish.

Yuki ran to him, ducking and weaving through the throng of tourists. Then she was right in front of him, dropping her carry-on bag at his feet and standing on tiptoes in her sneakers so she could kiss him.

"Declan." The word was breathy. Yuki's eyes sparkled, and she was so beautiful she hardly seemed real.

He picked her up and spun her around as his lips met hers. They kissed, her arms wrapped around his neck, every second like a perfect snapshot.

Declan nuzzled her neck as he set her back on her feet. "You're home now, Yuki. With me."

"I know," she replied with a gasp as he kissed the shell of her ear. "I know."

Epilogue

6 Months Later

Byron Bay, Australia

Seated at her desk, Yuki stretched her arms above her head and gazed out the full-length windows over the strip of pale sandy beach and ribbon of turquoise Pacific Ocean. It was a stunning view. From her office on the clifftops, she could see quite a way in both directions. There was the yoga class on the sand, which she sometimes joined. Maybe she'd go tomorrow and stretch out her spine. Someone had given her quite the workout last night. With a smile on her face, she packed up her folder and highlighters.

She'd just finished up some Byron area tour bookings and sent all the details to Sinead's assistant at the travel agency in Melbourne. Later, she'd be meeting with some Japanese businesspeople who wanted to run day tours in the local area, taking visitors fishing and hiking in the bush. They appreciated her ability to speak both Japanese and Australian English. Whenever she answered the phone by saying "G'day", it made them laugh.

She couldn't see Declan from here of course, although his office was just along the hall. It was in his luxury house, like her own office. Or rather, in *their house*, as he kept reminding her. She was home, with him. Yuki picked up her phone to text him.

Yuki: Morning tea time!

Declan: I bought you a lemon poppyseed muffin

Yuki: :)

Declan: See you in 5

By the time she'd plonked herself down on a barstool at the island countertop in the large open-plan kitchen, Declan had already set out a plate with a muffin and another with fresh fruit. He was busy making her an espresso coffee and taking his sweet time about it.

"The service in this cafe gets worse and worse. Lucky the barista's so handsome," she joked, then blew him a kiss when he turned around and flashed his movie-star smile.

Yuki studied Declan's face as he walked towards her. His blue eyes glowed almost as bright as the glimpse of ocean through the kitchen windows, and his wavy hair flopped over his forehead. It was a little long, but she loved it like that. She loved everything about him. Even dressed in simple dark jeans and a long-sleeved white shirt, he was totally swoon-worthy.

That's probably why her heart skipped a beat when he rounded the island and came up behind her. Or perhaps it was the way he turned her stool so he could lean down and kiss her, his lips lingering on hers like he was savouring a taste of pleasure. Then he wrapped his right arm around her and placed a small turquoise box on the plate in front of her, right beside her muffin.

Yuki gasped and covered her mouth with her hand she met his steady gaze.

"Yuki Yamimoto, my love, will you marry me?" Declan reached around and opened the box.

A shimmer of rainbows sparkled from the facets of the princess-cut diamond ring inside. She looked up at him. "Oh, wow. Yes, Declan. Of course I'll marry you!"

She swivelled round further on her stool, and he stepped between her legs, close enough to her body that the blood heated in her veins. He slid the ring onto her finger, and wouldn't you know? It fit perfectly.

"Good." He said the word like it summed up everything, and maybe it did.

Declan gripped her hips and leaned forward for another kiss. "I love you, Miss Yuki. Or should I say, Mrs Moriarty?" he whispered against her mouth.

Yuki sighed and nibbled at his lower lip. "Hmm. I quite like the sound of Declan Yamimoto. Or maybe we could hyphenate?"

"We can hyphenate all night long, darlin'." With that, he lifted her and, carrying her over his shoulder, fireman style, headed off towards the master bedroom. "I think we need a break from work today."

Yuki squealed and swatted Declan on his perfect butt. "Mine!"

His growl in response was a thing of beauty. Yes, he was hers. And she belonged to him too. Forever.

Yuki had always had a problem with billionaires. But lucky for her, Declan was only a run-of-the-mill, ordinary millionaire. Her millionaire. She liked that. A lot.

Read more

Take off and explore the Girl on a Plane series by Cassandra O'Leary!

Girl Under The Christmas Tree – A Holiday Romance Prequel Novella

Girl on a Plane series #0.5

Find out how Yuki and Declan met in this steamy holiday romcom novella. This story is an introduction to the Girl on a Plane series. Yuki Yamimoto isn't the kind of girl to say no to opportunity, especially when it comes swaggering into the five-star hotel where she works, dressed in a three-piece suit. Declan, the handsome wavy haired man with a movie star smile and charming Irish accent is almost irresistible . . . If only he wasn't a hotel guest! Maybe they could break the rules for just one night. Yuki's about to embark on a life full of adventure . . . but will she get to keep Declan as part of the package deal? She hopes so. It's her number one Christmas wish.

Buy now in ebook or paperback

Girl on a Plane – Cassandra O'Leary's award-winning debut novel

Girl on a Plane series #1

Meet Sinead and Gabriel as they are first thrown together during a flight to London. He's gorgeous but grumpy, she's 99% sunshine. Sparks and banter fly when this Aussie billionaire meets a bubbly Irish flight attendant who may just be his match. When they're together in Singapore during a typhoon, it seems fate has thrown them together. There's only one bed in the airport hotel, but a single steamy night could lead to more... if they can jettison their excess baggage and learn to trust.

Will love take flight?

Buy now in ebook, paperback and hardcover

Girl on a Babymoon – A steamy romance novella

Girl on a Plane series #1.5

Catch-up with Sinead and Gabriel, five years after they met in *Girl on a Plane*. It's their anniversary, and Sinead has a big surprise for Gabriel. But will he like her surprise? Or will it stress him out even more than usual? Sinead can't help being nervous, as lately it seems they've been like two flights going in opposite directions, barely passing each other en route to different destinations. This weekend at an island resort is a good idea, isn't it?

A romantic getaway and steamy role-playing feature in this laugh-out-loud story of a marriage in trouble, or maybe, a marriage that will be stronger than ever!

Buy now in ebook

Girl on an Island – coming June 2024

Girl on a Plane series #3

Bridie takes a new job as a marketing manager at a resort on a tropical island but she isn't expecting her brother's best friend from Ireland to be there! Now they're stuck together, and the temperature is rising . . .

Pre-order the ebook

Go to cassandraolearyauthor.com/books

Also by Cassandra O'Leary

Dating Little Miss Perfect

A 2023 new release, stand-alone romcom novel by Cassandra O'Leary. Perfect for fans of *The Love Hypothesis* by Ali Hazelwood and *The Soulmate Equation* by Christina Lauren!

On an anonymous online dating app, LittleMissPerfect meets HotAussie007 and it's love at first click. In real life, a smart but spiky woman in STEM, research scientist,

Dr Eden, meets a laid-back Aussie marketing manager, Finn, at the big pharma company where they both work in California. They're forced to compete for special projects funding, and both their jobs are on the line.

Eden just wants to win at science and in life. It's not happening! She can't stand Finn's too-cool-for-school, nice guy act, or his delectable forearms that keep invading her space. While Finn is stupidly attracted to Eden, when she's not telling him off, he isn't free to pursue her. He's stuck in the worst position in his professional life, and doesn't see a clear way out. He can't tell her the whole truth about what's going on at work or in his personal life... or it could all blow up in his face.

When they realise the truth about their online alter egos, dating is off the table. Can they ignore their inconvenient attraction, and work together to take down their unethical boss? Or will intense rivalry cause their IRL work lives and online love lives to collide and explode like a science experiment gone wrong?

Excerpt of *Dating Little Miss Perfect*

HotAussie007: Hi stranger. Talk dirty to me!

Eden heard her smartphone ding and knew who it was before she looked. She grabbed her phone. Yes, it was her anonymous *almost* boyfriend. Hardly anyone messaged her. And that tingly anticipation in her lower belly, no one else had that effect.

She shouldn't be doing this at work. It seemed naughty. A little dirty. But she was addicted to messaging him. As with any addiction, she couldn't help herself. Taking a deep breath, she straightened her pristine white lab coat and smoothed back a lock of hair escaping her high ponytail. Silly, considering they couldn't see each other, but she wanted to look her best.

Eden tapped out her response... No. *Delete!* She wouldn't go all the way totally sexy. Not at work.

LittleMissPerfect: Hey big boy, what's up?

HotAussie007: That's it? Nice dirty talk. You're a real bad girl LOL

LittleMissPerfect: I'm at work. Covert messaging in progress *side eyes*

She scanned the lab. Her fellow science geeks were absorbed in their work, some plugged into earbuds as they conducted experiments or typed up reports. Felicity, her research assistant, was focused on analyzing the drug assay.

All clear.

HotAussie007: I'm working too. Coffee break. What are you wearing?

LittleMissPerfect: Not telling. You have to guess. Some men fantasize about my prim and proper outfit. And what's underneath...

HotAussie007: Gah! Librarian? School teacher? Am I close? Stern, bossy, smart as a whip. I like this train of thought *daydreams*

LittleMissPerfect: I'm picturing you in underwear over tights. I've got this whole Clark Kent/Superman fantasy going on...

HotAussie007: *choke* Standard office gear today. Sorry to disappoint. But you can be my Lois Lane any day.

LittleMissPerfect: You're making me shy *blushes*

HotAussie007: Don't be shy. I like you.

Her belly flipped. *Likey like.*

HotAussie007: Will you meet me IRL?

Meet him? In real life? Her skin tingled, heat rising up her throat and across her cheeks. *Oh God.*

It could go spectacularly wrong, but she wanted to meet him. She wanted. Bad. All this online flirting had her mind intrigued and her body set to explode at the merest hint of a sexual fantasy. It was weeks since they'd ditched the dating site for one-on-one chats. But they'd kept things casual. And anonymous.

She'd chickened out of meeting him once already. Maybe she'd been smart. What if he took one look at her and bolted out the door? What if he didn't go for geek girls? What if she couldn't be sexy and funny in real life?

Eden loved the banter they shared online. But it was way easier to sex it up virtually with a faceless man than to flirt with a real, live, hot and sweaty human. Oh, but she wanted hot and sweaty.

Time to bite the bullet, to see if he was as funny and sexy as he seemed in their chats. She was dying to know what he looked like. Perhaps she'd indulge his librarian fantasy.

LittleMissPerfect: You're on. Sweep me off my feet, big shot. Get back to me with a time and place. I'll wear something strict.

HotAussie007: *dies* Will message later

Eden stared into space, indulging in her superhero fantasy. But Superman was too boring. This situation called for Thor. Lois Lane morphed into the spunky scientist Jane. With her long dark hair and subtle curves hidden under a lab coat, she did look a little like Eden. She'd help Thor save the world and hold on to his hammer... She'd happily oblige her hero. Strong, powerful, built like a pro wrestler but with a caring side. He'd do anything to protect her and save humanity.

As she was stroking her bare thigh near the edge of her summer skirt, a looming presence materialized behind her, sparking warning tingles across her nape, making the tiny hairs stand on end. Eden knew who it was. The man had timing. Bad timing. And he'd snuck up behind her bench in the open-plan lab. Was he trying to make her uncomfortable?

A few words rose to the front of her mind and they weren't polite. Eden tried to keep it cordial with the bane of her professional existence. "Donohue. To what do I owe the pleasure?"

She swiveled on her stool to face her work rival, and not for the first time, she wished Finn Donohue's looks matched his unpleasant personality. Instead, he had stunning sea-green eyes, tousled caramel hair, and over six feet of hunky height. All the muscles. None of it made him more appealing. It just didn't. Okay, his Aussie accent made him a tad more attractive. But only a little.

Odd how she was surrounded by Australians, online and at work. A little alarm went off in her brain but she ignored it. This particular Aussie was definitely annoying.

Finn heaved a long-suffering sigh. "You know why I'm here, at least you should. The final clinical trial report. It's three days overdue, Eden."

He leaned over her, drumming his fingertips on the bench, invading her personal space. She crossed her arms under her breasts, and his gaze tracked down to her V-neck for a second. Eden stared at him without speaking until he slowly blinked and met her eyes.

Her lips stretched in a mock-friendly smile. "It's *Doctor Robinson*. And as I said in my email, I'm still waiting on the blood test results from the LA lab. I can't magically make them appear on my desk here in San Diego."

Finn straightened. "Well, keep me updated. We need to get this drug to market ASAP, and I won't be held accountable if you don't deliver your end of the project."

Eden waved him away. "I get it. Now, shoo!" She must have scared him because he took a step backward. Smoothing down her skirt, she sighed. "Go back to your marketing cubicle. Relax in a beanbag chair and sip your hipster coffee. Send some tweets or whatever it is you do, and let the smart people do their jobs."

He narrowed his eyes. "Right. Wouldn't want to interrupt all that important texting, *Doctor* Eden." Finn shot her a glimmer-of-death glare, then turned and strode from the lab.

She did not admire his retreating form in his sharp suit. Broad shoulders, slim waist... firm butt. Nope, she scarcely noticed him.

Buy now in ebook and paperback

Short reads

Hot In The City: A Romantic Comedy Story Collection
Chocolate Truffle Kiss
Tree Love
Friday I'm In Love

Find out more at **cassandraolearyauthor.com/books**

About Cassandra O'Leary

C assandra O'Leary is an Aussie romance, romantic comedy and women's fiction author, corporate communications escapee, avid reader, and film and TV fangirl.

In 2015, Cassandra won the global We Heart New Talent contest run by HarperCollins UK and her debut novel, *Girl on a Plane*, was released in 2016. Cassandra was also a finalist in contests run by AusRom Today, Romance Writers of America and Romance Writers of Australia. She has since indie published several titles including *Dating Little Miss Perfect*, a romcom novel, and story collection, *Hot In The City*.

You'll find Cassandra in Melbourne, Australia, chasing her two high-energy mini ninjas and drinking excellent coffee with her superhero husband. She loves to read and her favourite romance and romantic comedy authors include Amy Andrews, Kylie Scott, Talia Hibbert, Cat Sebastian, Christina Lauren, Sally Thorne, Marian Keyes, Emily Henry, Lucy Parker and Alexis Hall.

Cassandra O'Leary is a proud member of Romance Writers of Australia, the Australian Society of Authors, and the Melbourne Romance Writers Guild.

Read more at **cassandraolearyauthor.com**

Acknowledgements

I owe a great deal of thanks and probably wine/cocktails/chocolate to my rockstar writer friends in the Melbourne Romance Writers Guild including Savannah Blaize, PJ Vye, Michelle Somers, Melanie Coles and some other writer friends from Romance Writers of Australia including Samara Parish and Justine Lewis. Thanks for listening to my mad ideas about a couple stuck together at a luxury resort, and understanding that for some reason there would be a monkey. Sometimes these things make sense eventually.

Thanks to my fabulous editor, Liz Dempsey, who sorted out my weirdo sentences, timeline issues (sorry, I thought there weren't any timeline problems in this one!) and deleted the majority of my superfluous exclamation marks.

I may have snuck some back in. I'm overexcited, just like my characters!

The amazing Deborah Bradseth designed the illustrated cover for this novella to match the overall style of the *Girl on a Plane* book cover but gave it a fresh, tropical look at the same time. Perfect, five stars, no notes.

Last but not least, thanks to my husband and kids who put up with me when I'm in last-minute editing and publishing mode. Mum goes a bit bananas when deadlines are looming upon her, and yes, I will finish the novella soon. Now, even. You're all very handsome with big biceps.

Playlist

**If you're wondering what songs Yuki and Declan
would listen to, here is the list!**

"Cruel Summer" by Taylor Swift

"Still Into You" by Paramore

"This Boy's In Love" by The Presets

"Think About You" by Ladyhawke

"Foreign Accent" by Molly Millington

"I Feel It Coming" by The Weeknd

"Into My Arms" by Nick Cave and the Bad
Seeds

"Nothing To Love About Love" by Peking
Duk x The Wombats

"Walking After You" by Foo Fighters

"I Want To Be With You" by Chloe Morion-
do

Printed in Great Britain
by Amazon